It's too late to screw it all up, right?

When this journal began in 1998, we printed its first issue, and the next twelve or so issues, at Oddi Printing in Reykjavik, Iceland. Around 2004, the exchange rate made it too expensive to continue printing there, but the folks at Oddi—Arni, Bjossi, all the pressmen in their blue jumpsuits—remained our friends. Given the dire economic straits Iceland finds itself in, we decided to print this issue, a throwback in terms of its design, at Oddi. We hope that you'll consider Oddi for your printing needs, as they and all manufacturers in Iceland need your help to dig themselves out of the mess their bankers, crazier than bankers pretty much anywhere else, made. ¶We've also returned, with this issue, to a Wells Tower story that originally ran in McSweeney's 23. Last fall, Wells rewrote "Retreat" from start to finish, switching the perspective from one brother to another, adding new angles and incidents, and now, in the spirit of alternate-universe episodes and classic-TV remakes, we are running the new one. It is as good as ever, and maybe better; for a more comprehensive explanation, we'll turn to Wells. ¶(This is his take, now, starting here:) Short stories always look really easy to write before you actually start writing them, and when an editor at McSweeney's wrote me asking if I had a piece of short fiction for an upcoming issue, I told him I'd have it for him in a week. Three weeks later, I told him it wouldn't be possible to write this story and that I was sorry and would he please leave me alone. ¶One thing that was screwing me up was all the long-form nonfiction work I'd been doing. Nonfiction—even "literary" nonfiction—calls for tools and processes that are pretty much useless when it comes to making short stories. In metalworking, they have this term, "cold connection," which is when you take two pieces of metal and a rivet. A few smart bashes, and you've got a bracelet with lots of nice bangles on it, and you've spared yourself the hot, tedious business of soldering and sweating joints. In a pinch, nonfiction can squeak by on cold connections. You go out and witness things, and if you've got at least a few compelling scenes, you can fuse them with the cold rivets of journalistic writing—the transition, the fraudulent hardware of arc and angle. Nine times out of ten the reader won't feel gypped, never mind that there's no real heart thumping in the thorax of your tin man. ¶Fiction can't be approached in such calculated fashion; at least I can't approach it that way and feel good about myself in the morning. But I'd been given a firm deadline for the story, so I started cold-connecting a bunch of spare parts I had laying around. I had an idea for two brothers who didn't get along, and an old man who would serve as a kind of ball joint between them, and also this story about a moose hunt for which I was trying to find a home. ¶(The moose story I'd heard from a guy named Clay Whitebear whom I met ten years ago during a job in a salmon cannery in Alaska. Clay was a long-term Alaska man, and one autumn he had a visit from his brother-in-law, a Californian, who was determined to go out and kill a moose. Clay knew what an ordeal killing a moose was. A good-size moose can weigh well above 1,000 pounds, and Alaska law requires you to take 80 percent of the meat, or they can lock you up for squandering the corpse. The day of the hunt was rainy and miserable, but the eager brother-in-law kept Clay out there all day. Finally, after eight fruitless hours, Clay convinced the other man that they should pack the project in. They'd just climbed into the boat when a moose walked out of the woods and the delighted brother-in-law shot it dead. So they dismantled it, an exhausting, gory affair, and just as they'd gotten the last haunch stacked, a second moose walked out of the woods. Before Clay could stop him, the brother-in-law shot that one, too. In the first draft of "Retreat," I borrowed the whole two-moose anecdote, and then deleted it. It astounds me, by the way, how much of the fiction writer's job involves finding ways for fewer things to happen.) ¶At any rate, after a few more weeks, I'd finally lashed together something that resembled a story. I had some conflict and some decent descriptions. The sentences were tidy enough. The old-man character, called "Bob" in that first draft, said a few desperately wacky things in hopes of getting the reader to chuckle. Yet when I sat down to give it another look before signing off on my collection of short stories, *Everything Ravaged, Everything Burned*, I read the first few pages and was horrified. After all the work I'd done on it, the story looked cheap and inadequate and shameful. Reading it, I suffered the breathless revulsion that some of us feel when looking in the mirror, thinking, "Oh my God. I can't believe that's my actual face." *(cont. on pg. 201)*

PFAFF II

by BILL COTTER

HE STATE HOSPITAL, viewed from above, was laid out like a swastika. I was on a unit on the second floor of the northeast elbow, Pfaff II. Or rather, I was in the Reflection Area, which was a part of a penal annex off of the main unit at Pfaff II, in which the aggressive, hypermanic, disobedient, suicidal, and just plain ornery folk were stabled to cool their heels, and to reflect.

Recently admitted question marks were also housed there. I was immediately confined, when they brought me in, to Reflection Room C. RRC.

I had a thin mattress and a blanket. No books, newspapers, plush toys, decks of cards. My brain juggled guilt and ideas and schpilkes. I counted, I hummed, I did sit-ups. I taught myself a rudimentary mnemonic system. I made up palindromes. Tums for a war of smut. I tore a little hole in the mattress and screwed it often. The days passed. Every five minutes a nurse peered in at me through the window in the door, which remained closed.

Eventually Dewey Martin stopped by.

"I *work* here, man," he told me, when I asked how he knew where I was. He looked and sounded transcendentally defeated. "Geriatrics. Word gets around."

"I don't like you to see me like this," I said, discreetly covering the hole in the mattress. Dewey had been a drinking buddy back in Boston. Not a close friend, really. "But I'm awfully glad to see you. How's the eye?"

Some months ago he and I had taken a beating from a barmate. I'd gotten away with a hairline crack in the jawbone, but Izzoli—the barmate—had gouged out Dewey's eyeball. Since then Dewey'd taken to wearing an eye patch with a Red Sox logo.

"Fine," he said. He was sitting on a plastic chair in the hall, just outside the door to my RR. He stared at me. Something about an eye patch redoubles the good eye's staring power.

"Listen—" I said, uncomfortable with his frankly assessing gaze. "Will you do me a favor? I haven't been able to—I've been hoping to talk to Leigh, actually. But I—I can't use the phone at the moment."

I paused. Leigh was the ebullient bartender at my old local hang-out. When you came in she'd wink and gesture in zingy semaphore until you felt like a celebrated wit and lover instead of a glum beer drone. I had been in love with her for a long time. She'd taken me in, once, just before I'd been brought to Pfaff, and I'd never said thanks. Dewey continued to stare.

"Jerome," he said. "Izzoli murdered her, man. Said she'd been with a guy. Stuffed her in her own refrigerator."

I stood up. "When!"

He shrugged. "It was a week or so ago."

I had nowhere to really go, but I tried to push past Dewey, just to go somewhere.

"Whoa, pal. Whoa. Nurse!"

The familiar thunder of furious orderlies rose in the hall.

Dewey visited a couple more times. He sat and smoked and conjectured mystical explanations for Wade Boggs's disappointing .261 average. We didn't talk about Leigh. Once, I asked him if he'd loan me some money so I could get some new socks and junk food at the commissary when I got out of this fucking room. He left sixty bucks at the nurses' station. He didn't visit again after that.

I had a neighbor, in Reflection Room B, who had been there since I'd been remanded. The only times I even knew she was there were when both our doors happened to be open and her dulled crying washed into the hallway. Otherwise there was no movement or sound from RRB at all. I occupied the long, prone hours rescuing Leigh in a thousand different ways.

After a couple of months they allowed my door to stay open during the day. Shortly after, they let me sit just outside my room on a plastic chair for five minutes, once an hour. A nurse had to be present, sitting across from me. It was usually Chuck.

Chuck dressed like Abe Lincoln, with musty black suits and silly shirts. His avocation was to loan himself out as a waving figurehead at patriotic spectacles. He had a watch fob and an unmustachioed beard that must've been hard to keep up. He was mean and condescending and talked like William F. Buckley Jr.

I couldn't wait for my five minutes, at first, but the breaks quickly grew tedious. I was feeling loose and hale and ready to rocket into a program of reduced psychiatric maintenance; subsisting on a mere three hundred seconds of false liberty each hour became a harrowing dither. Inside my room, I hopped and boxed until the appointed moment. Once outside I bounced and jittered and did low-altitude chair gymnastics, all the while peering desperately at my fellow inmates, two of whom seemed always locked in a kind of perpetual argumentative discourse involving baseball caps. Then Chuck would pluck his gold watch out of a vest pocket and send me back in.

One afternoon well into our routine, a minute or two after I'd emerged, Chuck checked his watch and stood up.

"Hey!" I said. "No way that was five, Chuck!"

But he ignored me. He walked to the RRB and unlocked the door. A girl came out and sat on the chair next to mine.

"Chesterfields?" Chuck said to her, not unkindly.

She nodded.

She wore an old cotton nightgown with a wide neck that fell off one shoulder and exposed her back, which was sparsely ditched with old measles scars. Thick and thin crisscrossed razor marks, hundreds and hundreds, darkened her arms and legs, interrupted in places with round spots that I recognized as cigarette burns.

Chuck handed her a plaid beanbag ashtray and a cigarette. He lit it for her with a fancy brass lighter that looked like C-3PO. She moved only her wrist, swiveling her hand to and from her mouth to take a drag. Her brown hair hid her face. I'd never thought cigarettes smelled good, but that one did—like kerosene and almond oil. She finished the smoke in less than two minutes. I thought she might put it out in the palm of her hand, but she just flicked it once and ground it out thoroughly in the ashtray, folding it over and mashing it with her thumb, putting some shoulder into it. Then she got up and went back into RRB. She must've had at least two and a half minutes to spare.

Chuck took out his watch again and looked at me.

"After you, my dear man," he said, gesturing grotesquely at the door to my room. "If you please."

"How about one more minute?"

"After you sir."

"Ten seconds."

"Sir."

"A micronanosecond?"

He didn't move.

I leaned forward.

"Chuck," I whispered, "who's my neighbor?"

He stood up straight and sucked air into his head—it was what he did when he was about to let some tyranny loose on somebody.

I went into my room.

I lay on my mattress. I bit one corner. I stood up and paced the perimeter of the room for a while. I stopped and put my ear to the wall I shared with the RRB. I heard nothing. It was an old building. The walls were foot-thick stone and mortar.

I lay on the floor and began to count.

If I started counting right when Chuck sent me back in, I'd usually be up to around 6,100 when it was time for the next break.

At 6,300 I got up and went to the doorway.

"Chuck! It's time!"

Down the hall, Chuck stood at the nurses' station doing something obscure with a clipboard.

"Chuck!"

He put the clipboard down and moseyed up the hall. I came out and sat in my chair. He sat down opposite me, took out a hankie, and set to polishing the end of one of his weird Civil War shoes.

"Chuck," I said, "how much longer, you think? I've been in this room awhile now, and I feel just fine. Not *too* great, you know, not *manic*, but not too down either—I don't want to hurt myself or anything. I think it's time for me to emerge."

"A matter for your psychiatrist, sir," said Chuck, who had interrupted his polishing in order to reorganize a cuticle.

"Yeah, I know, but don't you think I've made progress in here?"

"It is not for me to grade the advances and retreats of a guest's infirmity, sir," said Chuck. "That shall remain in the demesne of one's physician."

"Oh," I said. "Remain in the demesne?"

"Of one's physician. Correct."

Chuck stood up and let the RRB girl out. He shook out a Chesterfield and lit it for her.

"Hey can I bum a smoke from you?" I said.

She waved her hand, moving it only at the wrist. "Sure." Her voice was rough from disuse.

Chuck, unfazed, pulled the soft pack of cigarettes out of a vest pocket and lit one with C-3PO. He handed it to me, filter first. I held it between my thumb and forefinger like a guy in a breadline in the 1930s. I breathed in directly, like I was siphoning gas. It went down smoothly, with a pleasant, neat-Scotch burn. I exhaled like I'd come up from a dive.

I was a natural. The blood rushed to, or maybe from, my head. It brought to mind the moment the icy sodium pentathol is introduced to the vein.

"Thank you," I said.

I thought about saying "Watcha in for" or something but didn't. I smoked the cigarette all the way down and put it out in the ashtray under the chair, folding it over and mashing it to shreds like I'd seen her do. Then I went back into the RRC without saying anything else and without being told.

I lay down and counted 6,130 cigarettes, each a perfect white-and-Nilla-Wafer-colored cylinder, each handed to me one at a time by the girl from the RRB, her face hidden in her hair, long scars climbing from her neck all the way out to her fingertips. Then, from down the hall, the *scolp* of Chuck's watch snapping shut.

I sat down in my chair. The girl's door was closed. I asked Chuck if there were any orphaned cigarettes in the nurses' station. He said that there might be a carton of generic something-or-others that someone had left behind after their discharge about a year before.

"Can I have one?"

He got them for me. Dodds's Smooth Value
Cigarettes. That became my brand.

My neighbor's breaks began to coincide more often with mine. Her spirits seemed to be improving. She sat up. She tucked her hair behind her ear sometimes. We talked once. She'd been admitted four months before me and had gone right to the RRB. She'd never left, because she was a constant suicide risk. Her voice was deep and rattly, like she was narrating a hard-boiled book-on-tape. Over the weeks her posture changed from a slump to a relaxed sprawl. Instead of thoroughly smothering her cigarettes like she used to do, she had gotten into the habit of stabbing them out in one quick motion, leaving them smoldering in the ashtray.

A month later they let me out of the RR, but the girl remained.

After I got out of the RRC I found myself in the habit of checking down the hall every hour or so to see if my old neighbor was on a smoke break. Sometimes she was, with Chuck sitting across from her, waggling a pencil over a word game in the newspaper. She glanced my way sometimes. Once, she waved.

One night, a few hours after lights-out, I woke to a low, sustained howling that suddenly climbed to a ragged scream, and then stopped.

In the morning I asked the other patients what had happened, but no one knew, and the staff refused to tell me. I didn't see the girl in her plastic chair anymore.

Eventually I went down to the RRB and looked in the little

window. The room was covered in mattresses. On the floor, between two of them, was a form in a camisole.

A hard whack on my rear surprised me.

"Stay away," said Chuck, pointing at my Adam's apple.

"Did you just spank me?"

"Begone!"

I had become a heavy smoker, and enjoyed every second of it. In less than a week I'd smoked the whole carton of Dodds's Chuck had given me. It wasn't long before I used up all the money Dewey'd loaned me; I was reduced to bumming cigarettes from the other patients. I quickly used up all my credit with them, too, and was given no more, except by the friendless Gert Hodge.

Gert had killed her eighteen-year-old sister with a bowling ball while the girl napped in a hammock. Gert had been nine at the time and the object of abuse by her father, grandfather, and the selfsame sister. She had been committed to a life of hospitals, surviving in the shells of at least three personalities, one of which was thorny and murderous. At other times she was an infant who lay on the floor and wailed, eyes shut, kicking weakly. The third personality, a weary, cerebral crab cake, was the one that sponsored my cigarettes, at two cartons a week, in exchange for Scrabble whenever she requested it, which was fine with me, because I liked Scrabble.

We played in the dining room, where you could smoke except during meals. I sat at the end of a long table. To my right, if I leaned back far enough, I could see down the hall where the RRs were. The girl was never there.

*   *   *

Spring came around. I got better at Scrabble, though Gert still won two out of three. I studied her dictionary and memorized all the short words.

Gert got Merits from a man who visited once a week. He'd fallen in love with her while working as a nurse on the juvenile unit where Gert had been quartered when she was fourteen or so. He'd been fired after he'd been caught on his knees, crying on her shoes, begging her to marry him. She allowed him to come by, give her a hug, and leave four cartons of Merits on Wednesday afternoons.

One Wednesday I was sitting in the dining area across from Chuck, waiting impatiently for Gert and her suitor to finish up an especially lengthy farewell embrace. I had run out of Merits the night before and had been atremble with nicotine fantods ever since.

Chuck looked at his watch, then got up and went down the hall.

I leaned back. The girl in the RRB was there, in her plastic chair. Her hair was at least three inches longer. She had the same nightgown on. She was thinner. She had bandages on both arms, thumbs to elbows. I couldn't imagine how she'd cut herself in there.

I got up. Thirty yards down the hall, the girl lifted up her head and swept her hair behind an ear with her cigarette hand. I waved. She waved back. Even at a distance, I saw the tremor in her hand.

"Okay?"

She smiled, barely, eyes only, and lifted her cigarette up to show me that she was.

After that I became a Scrabble marshmallow. Gert docked me eight cigarettes every time I shifted my attention away from the game to check on the welfare of the girl down the hall, and eventually she cut me off altogether. I was obliged to start bumming cigarettes from the other patients again, this time being more careful not to overdo it. Gert found a new opponent, a recently admitted skate punk who thrashed her with neither effort nor mercy. I sat in a chair where I could see down the hall, watch their games, and smoke, all at the same time.

One afternoon, while I kibbitzed the two of them and awaited the girl's emergence, I heard a nurse call my name. I got up and went to the nurses' station, which was a green-glass room like an air-traffic-control tower, raised a foot or so above the rest of the unit. Charge Nurse Hrondl looked at me. I asked her what was up. She said *Nothing what's up with you?* I said, Didn't you call me? *Nup,* she said.

"Somebody called me," I said, then immediately wished I hadn't—it was the kind of honest mistake that was transformed, in the minds of charge nurses, into a symptom of combative delusion or some other kind of psychiatric demonstration.

"Are you certain, Jerome?" she asked, all her nursey sensors redlining.

I backed off as casually as I could, passing by the hall on my way. The girl was leaning out of the RRB. I glanced into the dining room.

Chuck was asleep—his head had settled back against a folded-up ping-pong table. He snored apneically.

"Hey," said the girl.

I went down the hall.

"Hi," I whispered. "Was it you who called me?"

"Yeah," she said. "I need to get out. I need to go home."

"I need to get out, too," I said.

"I'll die if I stay."

She took my wrists in her hands. She began to cry. Her own wrists were no longer bandaged. The fresh scars, big and rough, were marked with littler scars from the stitches and staples. The new scars wandered through the old ones like red-dirt arroyos. They were not razor scars.

She held me around the waist for an instant. Her body was cold and thin. Then she let go and went to lie down on a mattress under the barred window, facing away from me. I went over and put my hand on her shoulder, but she didn't move. She was so still and cool I thought she might have just died, but after a moment there was the merest flush of blood warmth under my hand.

I made it back to the dining room just as Chuck burst from his nap.

I started talking to Madox, the skate-punk Scrabble prodigy, about how much I hated it here. He was a tough kid, and had been in some kind of ancillary Irish gang that did little jobs for Whitey Bulger. He had scars like caterpillars on his face. His hands reminded me of driftwood. I told him I couldn't wait to get out—that I *really* couldn't wait. That I was thinking about running.

"Too bad you don't have privs," he said one afternoon. "You could just walk off. Get lost in the city. They'd quit hunting you after a couple of weeks."

"They'll never give me privs."

Madox leaned forward on the dining-room table, holding his head up with one hand, looking bored and sleepy. He had a cigarette hanging out of the corner of his mouth, which was something very, very few folks can do without burning their eyes.

I asked him how he'd get out if he had to. After a few moments of thought, he said he'd probably knot a few sheets together, tying one end to a leg of the big couch by the window in the TV room. Then he'd hide the coil of sheets behind the couch. When the time was right, when the nurses' station was locked and Chuck was asleep and the floats had just checked the TV room, Madox would pick up a chair and heave it through the window, like Chief did in *Cuckoo's Nest*.

"There're bars on that window," I pointed out.

"This isn't prison," said Madox. "They won't hold. I'll just throw the chair again if it doesn't work the first time. Then I'd throw out the sheet, climb down, and run. The perimeter fence is nothing, you can tell that from here. I can run a mile in five and half minutes. I'll be at my old girlfriend's house in Greenmont in no time. She likes that kind of shit. Escapes and holdups and speeding turn her on." He paused. "I think I might just do this. Want to come?"

"What if it doesn't work? They'll get you back and put you in the RR," I said.

"I'm not afraid of the RR," he said, taking the cigarette out of his mouth and burning a hole in a Styrofoam coffee cup. "Get some thinking done."

"What if they send you to Bridgewater?"

Bridgewater was the step down from Pfaff II. The bottom step. I'd known people who'd gotten committed there, but I couldn't think of anyone who'd come back out again. The possibility made him whiten.

"Well" he said, lighting another cigarette and getting out the Scrabble set. "You just can't worry about that."

"And look," I said. "I want to bust out the girl in the RRB."

"Oh," he said, smiling so his caterpillar scars bunched up. "I get it. This isn't about escape, is it? It's about love."

"It isn't about either one," I said, hoping he wouldn't ask me to explain myself. "But listen, she can't just climb down a sheet rope like Papillon. She *bit* her arms—tore out all the cables and veins and stuff with her teeth. She can barely get a grip on a cigarette."

"Okay," he said. "So I'll escape through the window, and you two just walk out the double doors."

*   *   *

The outer door to Pfaff II sometimes didn't close all the way, but stuck before the bolt fell. It wasn't really an issue, because the inside door was always locked, and if the outer door wasn't shut, an alarm went off when the inner door was opened. The alarm went off all the time. Nobody really paid it much mind. Doctors and nurses were simply asked to pull the outer door shut when they came or went.

A day after my conversation with Madox I snuck down to the RRB. The girl was sitting on a mattress in the corner with her eyes closed.

"Hi," I said.

She focused on me, then looked away as if her eyes were following a fly in the room.

"We're getting out of here," I said.

This time she looked right at me, and sat up.

"What?" she said, hoarse.

"A little past eight tonight, just after your smoke break starts, you'll hear a crash, a breaking window. Wait a second, then look out in the hallway. You'll see me at the end of the hallway by the dining room, you know, where I always sit and smoke?"

"Uh huh," she said. She was standing now.

"Wait at your door until you see Chuck run past me. Then come out as quickly as you can, and just follow me."

She nodded, her eyes wide for the first time I'd ever seen.

I gave her a rubber band. "Right after you smoke, put your hair up."

"I don't know if I can climb out a window."

"Don't worry. We're taking the stairs."

Madox and I played Scrabble. He was calm, but my knees bounced and my heart thrupped. I couldn't concentrate. Chuck came in, looked at the score, and smirked. Madox was sitting like I usually do, both hands supporting his forehead so his eyelids stretched.

The patients with privileges were coming back from dinner. Corey and Diane, Erwin Chambless, Mister Jiujee, Pammy, Tim Gueng, Mona Bronstein, Ted Felz, Gert. They were all pretty stable, or at least stabilized, so they got to go off the unit. And Gert had been on Pfaff II for so long that they had to let her out now and then.

Gert looked down at the score and made no comment.

"How was dinner?" asked Madox.

"Had pudding," said Gert.

Chuck had just begun napping in the corner of the dining room, his head leaning as usual against the folded-up ping-pong table, when he woke up with a start.

He squinted at his watch and yawned like a cave. He got up and went down to the Reflection Rooms.

Madox looked at Gert. She nodded. Then he stood up and walked down the hall to the TV room. A moment later, we heard a roar, like a straining powerlifter. A shattering.

Chuck was past us instantly, a determined gleam in his eye—he loved calamity and blood. When he was in full sprint down the hall, I walked out of the dining room and stood at the end of the hallway. The girl was there. Her hair was tied up with the rubber band. She looked like a different person. I smiled at her and held my hand up, palm out. She didn't move. There was another terrible crash. In the station Nurse Hrondl had gotten her door open finally and was walking quickly toward the TV room. Nurse Hrondl was the charge nurse and not about to run.

I motioned for the girl to come.

"Just walk with me. Stay on this side of me."

We came to the inner door. I pushed it open.

The alarm went off.

Nobody paid any attention—everyone had dashed into the TV

room, except the old-timers who had heard crashes and seen escapes and dodged shooting daggers of glass before.

I pulled the masking tape off the bolt of the inner door, where Gert had stuck it on her way back from dinner. The door shut behind us, and the alarm stopped. Then I pulled open the outer door, and peeled the tape off that bolt, too.

We walked out, down the stairs, and into a summer evening, just as the sky was darkening from indigo to violet.

The road was quiet. Old, feeble streetlights dropped yellow cones of light. There was no sound except a little wind in the massive pines, and backyard bug zappers that fizzed from time to time. The road had no sidewalk, so we walked in the grass above the curb, or in the street whenever forsythia grew across the path. We had escaped from Pfaff nearly two hours before.

"Why did you want me to put my hair up?" she asked.

"I thought you'd look a little different, in case people came after us," I said. "They'd be watching for someone with long hair."

She stopped under the next light and looked around on the ground. Presently she found a mangled steel washer. She picked it up, pinched a waist-high gathering of her thin cotton nightgown, threaded it through the washer, then pulled the cloth until the nightgown was cinched around her waist.

"Does it look like a dress?" she said, modeling. "Or a nightgown still?"

"A dress." She was terribly thin. "Well done."

Across front yards squares of living-room light shone, and sometimes the flickering gray-blues of TVs.

We did not talk except to warn each other that a car was coming. Once she said *Oh a little cat*, when one kitten, and then another and another, came out from a thick bed of ivy. We sat in the road by the curb and played with them for a minute. Then she put them back in the ivy and we walked on.

The road wound more and more sharply and the hills got steeper. There were denser trees, fewer houses, and long gravel driveways. It felt like we were heading east, toward Boston, but I couldn't really tell.

"I'm pretty sure we're heading toward Somerville," I said.

"Okay. Doesn't matter."

It was dark, but her nightgown glowed at the peaks of the creases. Her bare feet fell dully on the road.

"Where are you going to go?" she said, a mile or so later.

"I'm not sure. I'll see if I can stay with somebody for a while."

"What were you doing there? At Pfaff, I mean."

We were going up a long hill, and we were out of breath.

"I took off from another hospital, but got caught pretty quick. I didn't resist. You know when you're in, you want out so you don't have to deal with life in there, then you want back in when you don't want to deal with life out here?"

"I know."

"But that relief I get after going in or coming out is getting shorter and shorter for me," I said.

"What about now? Do you already want to go back?"

We were just over the top of the hill and could see a good way off. A diffuse orange dome glowed faintly in the distance. Boston.

"No. I don't."

"Let's never go back."

We walked for hours. We were in a valley of sorts again, with smaller trees and houses closer to the road. The glow of Boston was obscured by hills.

Every hour or so I asked her how she was doing barefoot. For a while she said okay or fine. But eventually she said she needed to rest.

I thought it must have been five in the morning. Still an hour or more until dawn.

To our right was a dark house. It had two newspapers in the driveway.

"What's today?" I said.

"Friday."

"I'll bet you two bits they're gone for the weekend. Let's sleep in the grass in the backyard."

She pointed to the garage door. It was open an inch.

"Let's get a room," she said.

I lifted the door. It went up a foot nearly soundlessly, then made a sound like a downshifting bus and jammed. We grabbed each other and held our breath for at least a minute. I couldn't hear anything because of the chugging blood in my head. But nothing came, and I let her go. We crawled under the door and lay in the middle of the oily floor, each with an old *Boston Sunday Globe* for a pillow.

In the morning we set out again. Toward noon, the landscape began to flatten out. We no longer hid when cars came.

"I know you've gotta be hungry," I said.

"I'm good," she said. "I could use a cigarette more than anything. And clothes."

The sun was overhead, and there was little shade, even with the dense trees lining the road.

"You know, I think I've been down this road?" she said. "I think it runs into Route 2, which goes straight to Arlington. We could hitchhike."

I didn't like hitchhiking, but I thought it'd be okay with two of us. She held her thumb out while I watched where she walked, making sure she didn't step on any shards. Only a few cars slowed down, and nobody stopped.

After about an hour we came upon a road-construction crew. Workmen stood by the side of the road among idling earthmoving equipment, looking smug and aggressive. None of them were working. All were big and had tanned hands. They all wore orange vests and hard hats. They watched us. The afternoon traffic was roaring past, and there was no way around their site—an orange net fence separated their work area from the deep woods. We had to walk right through, over cracked concrete and torn rebar and other jagged smithereens.

"You lookin' for a ride?" said one of the men, during a break in the traffic noise. A couple of the others laughed. I didn't look at them, and neither did my friend.

"No thanks," I said, but my voice was drowned out by a new wave of traffic.

I looked back. They were all still standing there. A few waved to us with effeminate flourishes. One of the men yelled, "I've only got room for her!" After a second, he added, "If she's got room for me!"

A couple hundred yards later I glanced back again. The workmen had forgotten us and had gone back to shirking duty and leaning on things. None of the traffic stopped for us.

Off in the umber-green woods I saw sparks of light. I stopped and watched.

"Hey," I yelled over the highway noise. "There's another road on the other side of these woods. See? Not as much traffic—wanna try it?"

The sun was lower, but hot on our necks. The shade would be a break.

"Okay."

We started through the dense pines and paper birch. The forest floor was soft and had no growth except mushrooms and fiddleheads. It was surprisingly cool. Almost cold, and dark.

"Do you see the cars up there?" I said.

"Yeah," she said. "Somebody's slowing down."

It was true. A car had stopped. Two men headed toward us. One waved and yelled, "You two okay?"

"Yeah!" I yelled back.

My body felt light. The girl and I held hands.

They were in their thirties. I remember thinking, *Adults, thank god*, though they weren't much older than me. They looked capable. It was so cold in the woods all I could think of was the hot sun by the side of the road.

Where are you two headed?" one of them said.

"Boston," I said. I noticed they were wearing white shoes. The kind nurses wear.

My friend stopped. I looked back to see her open her mouth to scream, but no sound came out.

"Weren't you in RRC last time?" said Dewey, sitting outside my room, RRB. He had switched to a Celtics eye patch.

"Yeah," I said, not bothering to sit up.

"You hear about the girl?" he said.

I didn't reply.

"Bridgewater, man," he said. "She won't do well there."

I rolled over to face the window. Dewey stayed for a while, complaining to nobody in particular about Reggie Lewis not getting picked for the All-Star Game. He smoked and smoked. We didn't talk about the girl anymore.

STOWAWAYS

by NICK EKKIZOGLOY

I'D ONLY BEEN down in Albany about six months when the flood came and washed it all away. This was south-of-the-fall-line Georgia, where the land dropped off flat. I was a lineman for the water, gas, and light there and pulling all-nighters on account of the tremendous storms they have in late spring. The town drew me in from Atlanta because I'd known a girl from Albany who said it was the best place on earth. I didn't see it ever, even after it was washed in pieces down to the Gulf of Mexico, but I figured if a beautiful girl from there thought that much of it, then that could only mean other beautiful girls would think the same and be so taken by the place that they'd spend their whole lives in Albany just waiting for an outsider to come in and join them.

For the most part, there was nothing to do on all-nighters but hang out and drink and play chess or tell dirty jokes. Francis, the second man on my shift, was the closest thing to a friend I had in Albany. He was a squat guy with meaty shoulders and an easygoing charm. On the weekends he'd mow the Oak Hill Cemetery all the way to the Flint River and afterward fish with a cane pole for redbellies. If you asked him how he felt about disturbing the dead and the mummies he'd say, "My family's out there, too. I just keep it lookin' nice for them."

He was always the one to pour the first shots on a late night. We would start off on hard stuff and get easier, Wild Turkey or Knob Creek to Gentleman Jack and Jägermeister. He'd have the hooch in little airplane bottles he bought at the ABC and we would shoot them straight. It was only me and Francis on our shift, so we would do a lot of shots. After we'd finished each one, we'd stand them up empty on the chessboard. Sometimes he'd bring pills.

We could do whatever we wanted because our boss and controller, the gridmaster, was in another room locked away by himself. He sat in front of a monitor all hours of the day just waiting for a red light to blink. We couldn't see the grid because he didn't trust us, but when a line went down, ticker tape would spew from our old printer with directions to the transistor. Most nights, if we had a call, we'd go driving and walk around Oak Hill afterward, just to phase out the sounds of electricity in our skulls.

So on one particular night about two weeks before the flood, Francis and I had finished enough airplane bottles to fill up a chessboard.

That's sixteen apiece. My king was Crown Royal and his was Old Crow.

"You get me in checkmate in three moves and I'll get my sister to blow you," he said. He was hunched over the table sweating, looking as red as a Florida sunrise.

"I get you in checkmate in three moves, I'll get your sister to blow *you.* Never gonna happen," I said.

"It's just about thinking hard on a move and then finding a reason to do it," he said. He lightened up in the face and pointed at a green bottle of Jäger. "Your knight here could go a lot of places and do a lot of damage, but staying put and protecting the home front might be a better move. It's up to you," he said.

He looked hard at my knight so I decided to use it to kill a pawn. I bumped that little Smirnoff pawn off the board with my piece and it flew down and ticked across the tiled floor. The hole the pawn left allowed me to put his Old Crow king in check.

When I looked over to see what Francis thought, he was capping a pill bottle and chewing tabs. He smiled at me, and through his teeth I could see smashed pink and white pills mixed like candy.

"You're fucked," I said.

"I know. Shouldn't have told you to use the knight," he said.

I knocked down the Old Crow bottle, claiming victory, and then tape fed out of our printer sending us to a downed line off Philema, near the zoo. I grabbed the radio so Francis couldn't answer and in a minute we were dragging our shit out to the truck and I was dumping bottles in the trash.

Around 2:30 a.m. I had Francis up in the cherry picker flailing around. This was a live job and I'd be damned if I was going to be the one in the bucket with a madman at the controls. Besides, he was the veteran, and as it turned out it was just a routine insulator replacement. Supposed to be a downed line, but that was just the call; sometimes the gridmaster got it wrong. Somebody'd call in and say their TV isn't working because of a downed line and next thing you know Francis and I'd be out there looking for sparks on the ground.

All I could see of him now was his concrete-slab shoulders over the bucket, working up and down. I had him up there in good, safe placement, far enough from a row of pines that if a spark caught he wouldn't go up in blazes. I remember the humming of the transformer harmonized with his mumblings sounded like a single note on a church organ.

"Careful, France," I called. The wind was throwing limbs into the road and the moon was a gray smudge through the pines. He tossed down a toasted squirrel and laughed like Satan after I dodged it. In his state he could hardly feel his hands, I knew. What would happen if his rubber gloves slipped off? Would he explode? I often imagined the dangers of the job being more sensational than they were, like my death could only occur in catastrophic fashion. I imagined heads melting and chests cracking open and shooting zigzags of lightning coming out of eye sockets and mouths. Francis and I would talk about how it was the most dangerous job on earth, being a lineman. In front of him I acted like it was awesome, but later on I'd think about all the fried squirrels and then about hitching out of state.

"Got it," he called down. "Let's grab some hooch. Man, you hear that?" I didn't at first. "Those screams. Sounds like the Devil's beatin' ole girl." I listened and heard something far off that came in and out with the wind.

"I think those are monkeys at the zoo," I said. I lowered Francis down. He was still whooping about the Devil and how God should fly in and beat his ass. "I think those are monkeys at the zoo on account of the storm," I said again.

"Pres, you wouldn't know the Devil from a monkey any day of the week," he said. I took silent offense at that and brought him down hard onto the ground.

*　*　*

An hour later we were at Oak Hill with a bottle of tequila and Francis was singing Spanish love songs. He kept repeating Santa Esmeralda this and that. We were shot-out and stomping all over the graves, trying to find our way to the river. Francis pointed out where "his clan" as he called it was buried, over on a hill near a statue that in the night reminded me of a power-line pole. I wondered if there was someone under there who'd exploded in a cherry picker. We passed by little bricks that substituted for larger headstones and I asked Francis, "Do you just go over these?" He looked down and felt for the stone in the dark.

"Oh yeah, those are generally just whoever. All on their own, you know. No clan or anything," he said. "The mower goes right over them clean."

We stumbled around in the damp grass while waves of thunder rumbled in the distance. It seemed like the worst place in the world right then, Albany. It was kicking up good and Francis was a native doing his part, downing hooch and chomping pills. In the quiet between bursts of wind and thunder I could hear the pill bottle open and close, plastic on plastic.

When we got to the river we sat down and made sounds. Francis did a siren, so I would do gunshots. If he did a seal barking, I would do a fog horn. I ate some pills and we passed the tequila. We laughed like we had just crawled out of the grave as old buddies and met by the Flint River to say fuck you to death. We were out of our minds hammered.

The moon appeared out of the clouds and blinked three times. I remember hearing a voice that said "Seek shelter, my sons" and then sirens. I looked over to see if Francis was making the sirens, but he was lying on his back. I could see the wet of his eyes so I knew they were open.

"Did you hear that," I asked.

"What, God?" he said.

"Yeah," I said. "What do we do?" He sat relaxed like an expert, feet folded in the grass.

"We let him save us," he said. I sat back and let my arms lie across my chest, like a mummy. The sky looked like the face of Jupiter. I imagined God blinking his eye at us behind it. I was fucked on pills. But inside I knew it was the hooch, I knew it broke down chemicals and made pills do shit like this. Atlanta had taught me about hooch and pills.

I looked over to Francis and saw his eyes were still open. I thought he was dead. I didn't move, though.

The truth was, that storm was the first of a two-week monsoon in south Georgia. Twelve days in we'd gotten about fourteen inches of rain, enough to break seven dams upstream. The water looked like a wall when it came in. The animals at the zoo all died, except the bears that could climb trees and keep their snouts above the water. There was a picture on the front of the Albany *Herald* of two dead giraffes that looked like weird, stretched-out deer. They were lying side by side, like concrete statues waiting to be taken to a miniature-golf course.

And Francis, he lost his mind on pills and hooch after volunteering to wrangle the coffins that popped out of the ground at the cemetery. A while later he blew his brains out in a car outside the water, gas, and light. He'd been on the front of the *Herald*, too, a few days after the giraffes, towing a wire cord spun through the bars attached to the caskets. In the picture, he was leading a train of them with a johnboat down to Cromartie Beach, where families waited to identify the remains again. It was like one of those pictures of Italy, with all the blue and red sailboats beached out on sandbars, except in this case the sailboats were colored mahogany and brass. Some kid's mom was a skeleton that got caught up in the ropes course at the community college. I heard she looked like a big white spider. It was like for a second we were all fancy people with dangerous lives in faraway places. But it was Albany, and it was happening to Francis, my friend. He asked me for help when it came down to him being the only one to go look for coffins and stowaway bodies. I had to turn him down for whatever reason. It seemed I had a hundred of them back then.

Sometime before his suicide Francis and I took a ride out to the Civic Center, where there were still dead fish in the parking lot. We smoked a joint, and did some pills. We were in his mom's blue Toyota, the one he blasted himself in.

"Every last line is down," he said.

"It's out of our hands," I said. "The Corps of Engineers has Albany now."

"I heard that an entire house is missing," he said. He puckered his mouth tight around an airplane bottle of 151 and finished it quick. His eyes watered afterward. "Like the Man himself reached down and grabbed the thing. The *Herald* said a math teacher was inside with a puppy."

"It's gonna be a busy fall, for sure," I said. "Power's out up to Macon. It'll take a month alone for road crews to hitch up new poles and another for us to restring conductors."

He looked at me. "You sound like an ass, Pres." He studied his pill bottle low between his legs, then lifted it up to me. When I waved it off he opened it and took one. "Fuck city work," he said. "Fuck electricity."

We sat for a minute while sand whipped up and powdered the car in swooshes. Nobody was outside.

"What're you planning to do, then?" I said.

"I've got obligations, Pres. I've gotta mow Oak Hill." He laughed and got out of the car, slamming the door harder than necessary. Then he bent over and picked up a rusted toy harmonica off the ground and blew the water out of it.

FURTHER
INTERPRETATIONS
OF REAL-LIFE EVENTS

by KEVIN MOFFETT

AFTER MY FATHER RETIRED, he began writing trueish stories about fathers and sons. He had tried scuba diving, had tried being a dreams enthusiast, and now he'd come around to this. I was skeptical. I'd been writing my own trueish stories about fathers and sons for years, stories that weren't perfect, of course, but they were mine. Some were published in literary journals, and I'd even received a fan letter from Helen in Vermont, who liked the part in one of my stories where the father made the boy scratch his stepmom's back. Helen in Vermont said she found the story "enjoyable" but kind of "depressing."

The scene with the stepmom was an interpretation of an actual event. When I was ten years old my mother died. My father and I lived alone for five years, until he married Lara, a kind woman with a big laugh. He met her at a dreams conference. I liked her well enough in real life but not in the story. In the story, "End of Summer," I begrudged Lara (changed to "Laura") for marrying my father so soon after my mother died (changed to five months).

"You used to scratch your ma's back all the time," my father says in the final scene. "Why don't you ever scratch Laura's?"

Laura sits next to me, shucking peas into a bucket. The pressure builds. "If you don't scratch Laura's back," my father says, "you can forget Christmas!"

So I scratch her back. It sounds silly now, but by the end of the story, Christmas stands in for other things. It isn't just Christmas anymore.

The scene was inspired by the time my father and Lara went to Mexico City (while I was marauded by bullies and blackflies at oboe camp) and brought me home a souvenir. A tin handicraft? you guess. A selection of cactus-fruit candy? No. A wooden back-scratcher with extended handle for maximum self-gratification. What's worse, *TE QUIERO* was embossed on the handle. Which I translated at the time to mean: *I love me*. (I was off by one word.)

"Try it," my father said. His tan had a yolky tint and he wore a shirt with PROPERTY OF MEXICO on the back. It was the sort of shirt you could find anywhere.

I hiked my arm over my head and raked the back-scratcher north and south along my vertebrae. "Works," I said.

"He spent all week searching for something for you," Lara said. "He even tried to haggle at the *mercado*. It was cute."

"There isn't much for a boy like you in Mexico," my father said. "The man who sold me the back-scratcher, though, told me a story. All the men who left to fight during the revolution took their wives with them. They wanted to remember more..."

I couldn't listen. I tried to, I pretended to, nodding and going *hmm* when he said *Pancho Villa* and *wow* when he said *gunfire* and then *some story* when it was over. I excused myself, sprinted upstairs to my bedroom, slammed my door, and snapped that sorry back-scratcher over my knee like kindling.

A boy like me!

You'll never earn a living writing stories, not if you're any good at it. My mentor Harry Hodgett told me that. I must've been doing something right, because I had yet to receive a dime for my work. I day-labored at the community college teaching Prep Writing, a class for students without the necessary skills for Beginning Writing. I also taught Prep Prep Writing, for those without the skills for Prep Writing. Imagine the most abject students on earth, kids who, when you ask them to name a verb, stare like you just asked them to cluck out a polka with armpit farts.

Literary journals paid with contributors' copies and subscriptions, which was nice, because when your story was published you at least knew that everyone else in the issue would read your work. (Though, truth be told, I never did.) This was how I came to receive the Autumn issue of *Vesper*—I'd been published in the Spring issue. It sat on my coffee table until a few days after its arrival, when I returned home to find Carrie on my living-room sofa, reading it. "Shh," she said.

I'd just come back from teaching, dispirited as usual after Shandra Jones in Prep Prep Writing told a classmate to "eat my drippins." A bomb I defused with clumsy silence, comma time!, early dismissal.

"I didn't say anything," I said.

"Shh," she said again.

An aside: I'd like to have kept Carrie out of this because I haven't figured out how to write about her. She's tall with short brown hair and brown eyes and she wears clothes and—see? I could be describing anybody. Carrie's lovely, her face is a nest for my dreams. You need distance from your subject matter. You need to approach it with the icy, lucid eye of a surgeon. I also can't write about my mother. Whenever I try, I feel like I'm attempting kidney transplants with a can opener and a handful of rubber bands.

"Amazing," she said, closing the journal. "Sad and honest and free of easy meanness. It's like the story was unfolding as I read it. That bit in the motel: wow. How come you never showed me this? It's a breakthrough."

She stood and hugged me. She smelled like bath beads. I was jealous of the person, whoever it was, who had effected this reaction in her: Carrie, whom I met in Hodgett's class, usually read my stories with barely concealed impatience.

"Breakthrough, huh?" I said casually (desperately). "Who wrote it?"

She leaned in and kissed me. "You did."

I picked up the journal to make sure it wasn't the Spring issue, which featured "The Longest Day of the Year," part two of my sum-mer trilogy. It's about a boy and his father (I know, I know) driving home, arguing about the record player the father refuses to buy the boy, even though the boy totally needs it since his current one ruined two of his Yes albums, including the impossible-to-find *Time and a Word*, and—*boom*—they hit a deer. The stakes suddenly shift.

I turned to the contributors' notes. FREDERICK MOXLEY *is a retired statistics professor living in Vero Beach, Florida. In his spare time he is a dreams enthusiast. This is his first published story.*

"My dad!" I screamed. "He stole my name and turned me into a dreams enthusiast!"

"Your *dad* wrote this?"

"And turned me into a goddamn dreams enthusiast! Everyone'll think I've gone soft and stupid!"

"I don't think anyone really reads this journal," Carrie said. "No offense. And isn't he Frederick Moxley, too?"

"Fred! He goes by *Fred*. I go by Frederick. Ever since third grade, when there were two Freds in my class." I flipped the pages, found the story, "Mile Zero," and read the first sentence: *As a boy I always dreamed of flight.* That makes two of us, I thought. To the circus, to Tibet, to live with a nice family of Moonies. I felt tendrils of bile beanstalking up my throat. "What's he trying to do?"

"Read it," Carrie said. "I think he makes it clear what he's trying to do."

If the story was awful I could have easily endured it, I realize now. I could've called him and said if he insists on writing elderly squibs, please just use a pseudonym. Let the Moxley interested in truth and beauty, etc., publish under his real name.

But the story wasn't awful. Not by a long shot. Yes, it broke two of Hodgett's six laws of story-writing (Never dramatize a dream, Never use more than one exclamation point per story), but he'd managed some genuine insight. Also he fictionalized real-life events in surprising ways. I recognized one particular detail from after Mom died. We moved the following year, because my father never liked our house's floor plan. That's what I'd thought, at least. Too cramped, he always said; wherever you turned, a wall or closet blocked your path. In the story, though, the characters move because the father can't disassociate the house from his wife. Her presence is everywhere: in the bedroom, the bathroom, in the silverware pattern, the flowering jacaranda in the backyard.

She used to trim purple blooms from the tree and scatter them around the house, on bookshelves, on the dining-room table, he wrote. *It seemed a perfectly attuned response to the natural world, a way of inviting the outside, inside.*

I remembered those blooms. I remembered how the house

smelled with her in it, though I couldn't name the smell. I recalled her *presence*, vast ineffable thing.

I finished reading in the bath. I was no longer angry. I was a little jealous. Mostly I was sad. The story, which showed father and son failing to connect again and again, ends in a motel room in Big Pine Key (we used to go there in December), the father watching a cop show on TV while the boy sleeps. He's having a bad dream, the father can tell by the way his face winces and frowns. The father lies down next to him, hesitant to wake him up, and tries to imagine what he's dreaming about.

Don't wake up, the father tells him. *Nothing in your sleep can hurt you.*

The boy was probably dreaming of a helicopter losing altitude. It was a recurring nightmare of mine after Mom died. I'd be cutting through the sky, past my house, past the hospital, when suddenly the control panel starts beeping and the helicopter spins down, down. My body fills with air as I yank the joystick. The noise is the worst. Like a monster oncoming bee. My head buzzes long after I wake up, shower, and sit down to breakfast. My father, who's just begun enthusing about dreams, a hobby that even then I found ridiculous, asks what I dreamed about.

"Well," I say between bites of cereal. "I'm in a blue—no, no, a golden suit. And all of a sudden I'm swimming in an enormous fishbowl in a pet store filled with eager customers. And the thing is, they all look like you. The other thing is, I *love* it. I want to stay in the fishbowl forever. Any idea what that means?"

"Finish your breakfast," he says, eyes downcast.

I'd like to add a part where I say *just kidding*, then tell him my dream. He could decide it's about anxiety, or fear. Even better: he could just backhand me. I could walk around with a handprint on my face. It could go from red to purple to brownish blue, poetic-like. Instead, we sulked. It happened again and again, until mornings grew as joyless and choreographed as the interactions of people who worked among deafening machines.

In the bathroom I dried myself off and wrapped a towel around my waist. I found Carrie in the kitchen eating oyster crackers. "So?" she said.

Her expression was so beseeching, such a lidless empty jug.

I tossed the journal onto the table. "Awful," I said. "Sentimental, boring. I don't know. Maybe I'm just biased against bad writing."

"And maybe," she said, "you're just jealous of good writing." She dusted crumbs from her shirt. "I know it's good, you know it's good. You aren't going anywhere till you admit that."

"And where am I trying to go?"

She regarded me with a look I recalled from Hodgett's class. Bemused amusement. The first day, while Hodgett asked each of us to name our favorite book, then explained why we were wrong, I was daydreaming about this girl in a white V-neck reading my work and timidly approaching me afterward to ask, What did the father's broken watch represent? and me saying *futility*, or *despair*, and then maybe kissing her. She turned out to be the toughest reader in class, far tougher than Hodgett, who was usually content to make vague pronouncements about *patterning* and *the octane of the epiphany*. Carrie was cold and smart and meticulous. She crawled inside your story with a flashlight and blew out all your candles. She said of one of my early pieces, "On what planet do people actually talk to each other like this?" And: "Does this character do anything but shuck peas?"

I knew she was right about my father's story. But I didn't want to talk about it anymore. So I unfastened my towel and let it drop to the floor. "Uh-oh," I said. "What do you think of this plot device?"

She looked at me, down, up, down. "We're not doing anything until you admit your father wrote a good story."

"*Good*? What's that even mean? Like, can it fetch and speak and sit?"

"Good," Carrie repeated. "It's executed as vigorously as it's conceived. It isn't false or pretentious. It doesn't jerk the reader around to no effect. It lives by its own logic. It's poignant without trying too hard."

I looked down at my naked torso. At some point during her litany, I seemed to have developed an erection. My penis looked all eager, as if it wanted to join the discussion, and unnecessary. "In that case," I said, "I guess he wrote one good story. Do I have to be happy about it?"

"Now I want you to call him and tell him how much you like it."

I picked up the towel, refastened it, and started toward the living room.

"I'm just joking," she said. "You can call him later."

Dejected, I followed Carrie to my room. She won, she always won. I didn't even feel like having sex anymore. My room smelled like the bottom of a pond, like a turtle's moistly rotting cavity. She lay on my bed, still talking about my father's story. "I love that little boy in the motel room," she said, kissing me, taking off her shirt. "I love how he's still frowning in his sleep."

I never called my father, though I told Carrie I did. I said I called and congratulated him. "What's his next project?" she asked. Project! As if he was a famous architect or something. I said he's considering a number of projects, each project more poignant-without-trying-too-hard than the project before it.

He phoned a week later. I was reading my students' paragraph essays, feeling my soul wither with each word. The paragraphs were in response to a prompt: "Where do you go to be alone?" All the students, except one, went to their room to be alone. The exception was Daryl Ellington, who went to his rom.

"You sound busy," my father said.

"Just getting some work done," I said.

We exchanged postcard versions of our last few weeks. I'm fine, Carrie's fine. He's fine, Lara's fine. I'd decided I would let him bring up the journal.

"Been writing," he said.

"Here and there. Some days it comes, some days it doesn't."

"I meant me," he said, then slowly he paddled through a summary of how he'd been writing stories since I sent him one of mine (I'd forgotten this), and of reading dozens of story collections, and then of some dream he had, then, *finally*, of having his story accepted for publication (and two others, forthcoming). He sounded chagrined by the whole thing. "I told them to publish it as Seth Moxley but lines must've gotten crossed," he said. "Anyway, I'll put a copy in the mail today. If you get a chance to read it, I'd love to hear what you think."

"What happened to scuba diving?" I asked.

"I still dive. Lara and I are going down to the Pennecamp next week."

"Right, but—writing's not some hobby you just dabble in, Dad. It's not like scuba diving."

"I didn't say it was. You're the one who brought up diving." He inhaled deeply. "Why do you always do this?"

"Do what?"

"Make everything so damn difficult. I had to drink two glasses of wine before I called, just to relax. You were such an easygoing kid, you know that? Your mom used to call you Placido. I'd wake up panicked in the middle of the night and run to check on you, because you didn't make any noise."

"Maybe she was talking about the opera singer," I said.

Pause, a silent up-grinding of gears. "You don't remember much about your mother, do you?"

"A few things," I said.

"Her voice?"

"Not really."

"She had a terrific voice."

I didn't listen to much after that. Not because I'd already heard it, though I had—I wanted to collect a few things I remembered about her, instead of listening to his version again. Not facts or adjectives or secondhand details, but… qualities. Spliced-together images I could summon without words: her reaching without looking to take my hand in the street, the pockmarks on her wrist from the pins inserted when she broke her arm, her laughing, her crying, her warmth muted, her gone, dissolving room-by-room from our house. I'd never been able to write about her, not expressly. Whenever I tried she emerged all white-robed and beatific, floating around, dispensing wisdom, laying doomed hands on me and everyone. Writing about her was imperfect remembering; it felt like a second death. I was far happier writing about fathers making sons help drag a deer to the roadside, saying, "Look into them fogged-up eyes. Now that's death, boy."

"She always had big plans for you," my father was saying. It was something he often said. I never asked him to be more specific.

It occurs to me that I'm breaking two of Hodgett's laws here. Never write about writing, and Never dramatize phone conversations.

Put characters in the same room, he always said. See what they do when they can't hang up. "We'd love to see Carrie again," my father said after a while. "Any chance you'll be home for Christmas?"

Christmas was two months away. "We'll try," I told him.

After hanging up, I returned to my students' paragraphs, happy to marinate for a while in their simple insight. *My room is the special place*, Monica Mendez wrote. *Everywhere around me are shelfs of my memory things.*

Imagine a time for your characters, Hodgett used to say, when things might have turned out differently. Find the moment a choice was made that made other choices impossible. Readers like to see characters making choices.

She died in May. A week after the funeral my father drives me and three friends to a theme park called Boardwalk and Baseball. He probably hopes it'll distract us for a few hours. All day long my friends and I ride roller coasters, take swings in the batting cage, eat hot dogs. I toss a ping-pong ball into a milk bottle and win a T-shirt. I can't even remember what kind of T-shirt it was, but I remember my glee after winning it.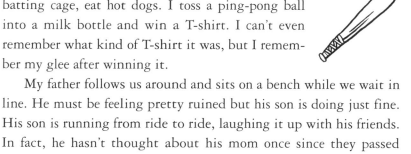

My father follows us around and sits on a bench while we wait in line. He must be feeling pretty ruined but his son is doing just fine. His son is running from ride to ride, laughing it up with his friends. In fact, he hasn't thought about his mom once since they passed through the turnstiles.

My father is wearing sunglasses, to help with his allergies, he says. His sleeves are damp. I think he's been crying. "Having fun?" he keeps asking me.

I am, clearly I am. Sure, my mom died a week ago, but I just won a new T-shirt and my father gave each of us twenty dollars and the line to the Viper is really short and the sun is shining and I think we saw the girl from *Who's the Boss*, or someone who looks a lot like her, in line at the popcorn cart.

I cringe when I remember this day. I want to revise everything. I want to come down with food poisoning, or lose a couple of fingers on the Raptor, something to mar the flawless good time I was having. Now I have to mar it in memory, I have to remember it with a black line through it.

"I'm glad you had fun," my father says on the drive home.

Our house is waiting for us when we get back. The failing spider plants on the front porch, the powder-blue envelopes in the mailbox.

November was a smear. Morning after morning I tried writing but instead played Etch-a-Sketch for two hours. I wrote a sentence. I waited. I stood up and walked around, thinking about the sentence. I leaned over the kitchen sink and ate an entire sleeve of graham crackers. I sat at my desk and stared at the sentence. I deleted it and wrote a different sentence. I returned to the kitchen and ate a handful of baby carrots. I began wondering about the carrots, so I dialed the toll-free number on the bag and spoke to a woman in Bakersfield, California.

"I would like to know where baby carrots come from," I said.

"Would you like the long version or the short version?" the woman asked.

For the first time in days I felt adequately tended to. "Both," I said.

The short version: baby carrots are adult carrots cut into smaller pieces.

I returned to my desk, deleted my last sentence, and typed, "Babies are adults cut into smaller pieces." I liked this. I knew it would make an outstanding story, one that would win trophies and change the way people thought about fathers and sons if only I could find another three hundred or so sentences to follow it. But where were they?

A few weeks after my father sent me his first story, I received the Winter issue of *The Longboat Quarterly* with a note: *Your father really wants to hear back from you about his story. He thinks you hated it. You didn't hate it, did you? XO, Lara.* No, Lara, I didn't. And I probably wouldn't hate this one, though I couldn't read past the title, "Blue Angels," without succumbing to the urge to sidearm the journal under my sofa (it took me four tries). I already knew what it was about.

Later, I sat next to Carrie on the sofa while she read it. Have you ever watched someone read a story? Their expression is dim and tentative at the beginning, alternately surprised and bewildered during the middle, and serene at the end. At least Carrie's was then.

"Well," she said when she was done. "How should we proceed?"

"Don't tell me. Just punch me in the abdomen. Hard."

I pulled up my shirt, closed my eyes, and waited. I heard Carrie close the journal, then felt it lightly smack against my stomach.

I read the story in the tub. Suffice it to say, it wasn't what I expected.

As a kid I was obsessed with fighter planes. Tomcats, Super Hornets, anything with wings and missiles. I thought the story was going to be about my father taking me to see the Blue Angels, the U.S. Navy's flight team. It wouldn't have been much of a story: miserable heat, planes doing stunts, me in the autograph line for an hour, getting sunburned, and falling asleep staring at five jets on a poster as we drove home.

The story is about a widowed father drinking too much and deciding he needs to clean the house. He goes from room to room dusting, scrubbing floors, throwing things away. The blue angels are a trio of antique porcelain dolls my mother held on to from childhood. The man throws them away, then regrets it as soon as he hears the garbage truck driving off. The story ends with father and son at the dump, staring across vast hillocks of trash, paralyzed.

I remembered the dump, hot syrup stench, blizzard of birds overhead. He told me it was important to see where our trash ended up.

When I finished, I was sad again, nostalgic, and wanting to call my father. Which I did after drying off. Carrie sat next to me on the sofa with her legs over mine. "What are you doing?" she asked. I dialed the number, waited, listened to his answering-machine greeting—*Fred and Lara can't believe we missed your call*—and then hung up.

"Have I ever told you about when I saw the Blue Angels?" I asked Carrie.

"I don't think so."

"Well, get ready," I said.

I quit writing for a few weeks and went out into the world. I visited the airport, the beach, a fish camp, a cemetery, a sinkhole. I collected evidence, listened, tried to see past my impatience to the blood-radiant heart of things. I saw a man towing a woman on the handlebars of a beach cruiser. They were wearing sunglasses. They were poor. They were in love. I heard one woman say to another: *Everyone has a distinct scent, except me. Smell me, I don't have any scent.*

At the cemetery where my mother was buried, I came upon an old man lying very still on the ground in front of a headstone. When I walked by, I read the twin inscription. RUTH GOODINE 1920–1999, CHARLES GOODINE 1923–. "Don't mind me," the man said as I passed.

At my desk, I struggled to make something of this. I imagined what happened before and after. What moment made other moments impossible. He had come to the cemetery to practice for eternity. I could still picture him lying there in his gray suit, but the before and after were murky. Before, he'd been on a bus, or car, or taxi. Afterward he would definitely go to... the supermarket to buy... lunch meat?

"Anything worth saying," Hodgett used to declare, "is unsayable. That's why we tell stories."

I returned to the cemetery. I walked from one end to the other, from the granite cenotaphs to the unmarked wooden headstones. Then I walked into the mausoleum and found my mother's placard, second from the bottom. I had to kneel down to see it. Another of Hodgett's six laws: Never dramatize a funeral or a trip to the cemetery. Too melodramatic, too obvious. I sat against something called the Serenity Wall and watched visitors mill in and out. They looked more inconvenienced than sad. My father and I used to come here, but at some point we quit. Afterward we'd go to a diner and he would say, "Order anything you want, anything," and I would order what I always ordered.

A woman with a camera asked if I could take her picture in front of her grandmother's placard. I said, "One, two, three, smile," and snapped her picture.

When the woman left, I said some things to my mom, all melodramatic, all obvious. In the months before she died, she talked about death like it was a long trip she was taking. She would watch over me, she said, if they let her. "I'm going to miss you," she said, which hadn't seemed strange until now. Sometimes I hoped she was watching me, but usually it was too terrible to imagine. "Here I am," I told the placard. I don't know why. It felt good so I said it again.

"Why don't you talk about your mom?" Carrie asked me after I told her about going to the cemetery.

"You mean in general, or right now?"

Carrie didn't say anything. She had remarkable tolerance for waiting.

"What do you want to know?" I asked.

"Anything you tell me."

I forced a laugh. "I thought you were about to say, 'Anything you tell me is strictly confidential.' Like in therapy. Isn't that what they tell you in therapy?"

For some reason I recalled my mother at the beach standing in the knee-deep water with her back to me. Her pants are wet to the waist and any deeper and her shirt will be soaked, too. I wondered why I needed to hoard this memory. Why did this simple static image seem like such a rare coin?

"Still waiting," Carrie said.

My father published two more stories in November, both about a man whose wife is dying of cancer. He had a weakness for depicting dreams, long, overtly symbolic dreams, and I found that the stories themselves read like dreams, I suffered them like dreams, and after a while I forgot I was reading. Like my high-school band teacher used to tell us, "Your goal is to stop seeing the notes." This never happened to me, every note was a seed I had to swallow, but now I saw what he meant.

Toward the end of the month, I was sick for a week. I canceled class and lay in bed, frantic with half-dreams. Carrie appeared, disappeared, reappeared. I picked up my father's stories at random and re-read paragraphs out of order. I looked for repeated words, recurring details. One particular sentence called to me, from "Under the Light."

That fall the trees stingily held on to their leaves.

In my delirium, this sentence seemed to solve everything. I memorized it. I chanted it. *I* was the tree holding on to its leaves, but I couldn't let them go, because if I did I wouldn't have any more leaves. My father was waiting with a rake because that was his *job* but I was being too stingy and weren't trees a lot like people?

I got better.

The morning I returned to class, Jacob Harvin from Prep Writing set a bag of Cheetos on my desk. "The machine gave me two by accident," he said.

I thanked him and began talking about subject-verb agreement. Out of the corner of my eye, I kept peeking at the orange Cheetos bag and feeling dreadful gratitude. "Someone tell me the subject in this sentence," I said, writing on the board. *"The trees of Florida hold on to their leaves."*

Terrie Inal raised her hand. "You crying, Mr. Moxley?" she asked.

"No, Terrie," I said. "I'm allergic to things."

"Looks like you're crying," she said. "You need a moment?"

The word *moment* did it. I let go. I wept in front of the class while they looked on horrified, bored, amused, sympathetic. "It's just, that was so *nice*," I explained.

Late in the week, my father called and I told him I was almost done with one of his stories. "Good so far," I said. Carrie suggested I quit writing for a while, unaware that I already had. I got drunk and broke my glasses. Someone wrote *Roach* with indelible marker on the hood of my car.

* * *

One day, I visited Harry Hodgett in his office. I walked to campus with a bagged bottle of Chivas Regal, his favorite, practicing what I'd say. Hodgett was an intimidating figure. He enjoyed playing games with you.

His door was open, but the only sign of him was an empty mug next to a student story. I leaned over to see *S.B.N.I.* written in the margin in Hodgett's telltale blue pen—it stood for *Sad But Not Interesting*—then I sat down. The office had the warm, stale smell of old books. Framed pictures of Hodgett and various well-known degenerates hung on the wall.

"This ain't the petting zoo," Hodgett said on his way in. He was wearing sweatpants and an Everlast T-shirt with frayed cut-off sleeves. "Who are you?"

Hodgett was playing one of his games. He knew exactly who I was. "It's me," I said, playing along. "Moxley."

He sat down with a grunt. He looked beat-up, baffled, winded, which meant he was in the early days of one of his sober sprees. "Oh yeah, Moxley, sure. Didn't recognize you without the... you know."

"Hat," I tried.

He coughed for a while, then lifted his trash can and expectorated into it. "So what are you pretending to be today?" he asked, which was Hodgett code for "So how are you doing?"

I hesitated, then answered, "Bamboo," a nice inscrutable thing to pretend to be. He closed his eyes, leaned his head back to reveal the livid scar under his chin, which was Hodgett code for "Please proceed." I told him all about my father. Knowing Hodgett's predilections, I exaggerated some things, made my father sound more abusive. Hodgett's eyes were shut, but I could tell he was listening by the way his face ticced and scowled. "He sends the stories out under my name," I said. "I haven't written a word in over a month."

To my surprise, Hodgett opened his eyes, looked at me as if he'd just awoken, and said, "My old man once tried to staple-gun a dead songbird to my scrotum." He folded his arms across his chest. "Just facts, not looking for pity."

I remembered reading this exact sentence—*staple-gun, songbird, scrotum*—then I realized where. "That happened to Moser," I said, "at the end of your novel *The Hard Road.* His dad wants to teach him a lesson about deprivation."

"That wasn't a novel, Chief. That was first-person *life*." He huffed hoarsely. "All this business about literary journals and phone calls and hurt feelings, it's just not compelling. A story needs to sing like a wound. I mean, put your father and son in the same room together. Leave some weapons lying around."

"It isn't a story," I said. "I'm living it."

"I'm paid to teach students like you how to spoil paper. Look at me, man—I can barely put my head together." His face went through a series of contortions, like a ghoul in a mirror. "You want my advice," he said. "Go talk to the old man. Life ain't an opera. It's more like a series of commercials for things we have no intention of buying."

He narrowed his eyes, studying me. His eyes drooped; his mouth had white film at the corners. His nose was netted with burst capillaries.

"What happened to the young woman, anyway?" Hodgett asked. "The one with the nasty allure."

"You mean Carrie? My girlfriend?"

"Carrie, yeah. I used to have girlfriends like Carrie. They're fun." He closed his eyes and with his right hand began casually kneading his crotch. "She did that story about the burn ward."

"Carrie doesn't write anymore," I said, trying to break the spell.

"Shame," Hodgett said. "Well, I guess that's how it goes. Talent realizes its limitations and gives up while incompetence keeps plugging away until it has a book. I'd take incompetence over talent in a street fight any day of the week."

I picked up the Chivas Regal bottle and stood to leave. I studied the old man's big noisy battered redneck face. He was still fondling himself. I wanted to say something ruthless to him. I wanted my words to clatter around in his head all day, like his words did in mine. "Thanks," I said.

He nodded, pointed to the bottle. "You can leave that anywhere," he said.

Another memory: my mother, father, and me in our living room. I am eight years old. In the corner is the Christmas tree, on the wall are three stockings, on the kitchen table is a styrofoam-ball snowman. We're about to open presents. My father likes to systematically inspect his to figure out what's inside. He picks up a flat parcel wrapped in silver paper, shakes it, turns it over, holds it to his ear, and says, "A book." He sets it on his lap and closes his eyes. "A... autobiography."

He's right every time.

My mother wears a yellow bathrobe and sits under a blanket. She's cold again. She's sick but I don't know this yet. She opens her presents distractedly, saying *wow* and *how nice* and neatly folding the wrapping paper in half, then in quarters, while I tear into my gifts one after another. I say thanks without looking up.

This year, she and I picked out a new diver's watch for my father, which we wait until all the presents have been opened to give him.

We've wrapped it in a small box and then wrapped that box inside a much larger one.

I set it in front of him. He looks at me, then her. He lifts the box. "Awfully light." He shakes it, knocks on each of the box's six sides. "Things are not what they seem."

My mother begins coughing, softly at first—my father pauses, sets his hands flat atop the box—then uncontrollably, in big hacking gusts. I bring her water, which she drinks, still cough-ing. My father helps her to the bathroom and I can hear her in there, gagging and hacking. For some rea-son I'm holding the remote control to the television.

The box sits unopened in the living room for the rest of the day. At night, with Mom in bed and me brushing my teeth, he picks it up, says "Diver's watch, waterproof up to a hundred meters," then opens it.

Carrie and I drove to Vero Beach the day before Christmas Eve. There seemed to be a surplus of abandoned cars and dead animals on the side of the road and, between this and the gray sky and the homemade signs marking off the fallow farms—PREPARE FOR THE RAPTURE; PRAISE HIM—I began to daydream about the apocalypse. I was hoping it would arrive just like this, quietly, without much warning or fanfare.

"I know it's fiction," Carrie was saying, referring to my father's most recent story, "but it's hard not to read it as fact. Did you actu-ally tape pictures of your mom to the front door when Lara came over the first time?"

"Maybe," I said. "Probably. I don't really remember."

I taped the pictures in a circle, like the face of a clock. I waited at the top of the stairs for the doorbell to ring.

Carrie pointed to a billboard featuring the likeness of a recently killed NASCAR driver's car, flanked by white angel wings. "I hope they haven't started letting race cars into heaven," she said.

I finally talked to my father about his writing while we were in the garage looking for the styrofoam-ball snowman. We were searching through boxes, coming across yearbooks, macramé owls, clothes, and my oboe, snug in purple velvet. I always forgot how fit and reasonable-looking my father was until I saw him in person. His hair was now fully gray and his silver-rimmed reading glasses sat low on his nose.

"I didn't know we went to the dump to hunt for those dolls," I said. It sounded more reproachful than I meant it to.

He looked up from the box, still squinting, as if he'd been searching dark, cramped quarters. "You mean the story?"

"'Blue Angels,'" I said. "I read it. I read all of them, actually."

"That's surprising," he said, folding the flaps of the box in front of him. "Best not to make too much out of what happens in stories, right?"

"But you were looking for those dolls."

"I didn't expect to find them. I wanted to see where they ended up." He shook his head. "It's hard to explain. After your mom died—I'd be making breakfast and my mind would wander to Annie and I'd start to lose it. The only time I relaxed was when I slept. That's why I started studying dreams. I found that if I did a few exercises before falling asleep, I could dictate what I dreamed about. I could remember. I could pause and fast-forward and rewind. You're giving me a 'how pitiful' look."

"It's just strange," I said. "The dreams, the stories, it feels like

I haven't been paying attention. I had no idea you were being all quietly desperate while I was waiting for my toast."

"It wasn't all the time." He pushed his glasses up on his nose and looked at me. "You should try writing about her, if you haven't already. You find yourself unearthing all sorts of things. Stories are just like dreams."

Something about his advice irritated me. It brought to mind his casually boastful author's note, *This is his first published story.* "Stories aren't dreams," I said.

"They're not? What are they, then?"

I didn't know. All I knew was that if he thought they were dreams, then they had to be something else. "They're jars," I said. "Full of bees. You unscrew the lid and out come the bees."

"All right," he said, moving the box out of his way. "But I still think you should try writing about her. Even if it means the bees coming out."

We searched until I found the snowman resting face-down in a box of embroidered tablecloths. A rat or weasel had eaten half of his head, but he still smiled his black-beaded smile.

"I remember when you made that," my father said.

I did, too. That is, I remembered *when* I made it, without remembering the actual making of it. I made it with my mom when I was three. Every year it appeared in the center of the kitchen table and every year she would say, "You and I made that. It was raining outside and you kept saying, 'Let's go stand in the soup.'" Maybe she thought that if she reminded me enough, I'd never forget the day we made it, and maybe I didn't, for a while.

I brought the snowman into the house and showed it to Carrie, who was sitting in the living room with Lara. "Monstrous," Carrie said.

Lara was looking at me significantly. An unfinished popcorn

string dangled from her lap. "Carrie was sharing her thoughts on your dad's stories," she said. "Do you want to add anything?"

My father walked into the living room holding two mismatched candlesticks.

"They," I said slowly, looking at Carrie, waiting for her to mouth the words, "were," she really was lovely, not just lovely looking, but lovely, "good." I breathed and said, "They were good."

Carrie applauded. "He means it, too," she said. "That slightly nauseous look on his face, that's sincerity." Then to me: "Now that wasn't so hard. Don't you feel light now, the weight lifted?"

I felt as if I'd swallowed a stone. I felt it settling and the moss starting to cover it.

"Frederick here's the real writer," my father said. "I'm just dabbling."

How humble, right? How wise and fatherly and kind. But I know what he meant: Frederick here's the fraud. He's the hack ventriloquist. I'm just dabbing at his wounds.

What more should be said about our visit? I want to come to my father's Mexico story without too much flourish. I hear Hodgett's voice: Never end your story with a character realizing something. Characters shouldn't realize things: readers should. But what if the character is also a reader?

We decorated the tree. We strung lights around the sago palms in the front yard. We ate breakfast in an old sugar mill and, from the pier, saw a pod of dolphins rising and rolling at dawn. I watched my father, tried to resist the urge to catalog him. His default expression was benign curiosity. He and Lara still held hands. They finished each other's sentences. They seemed happy. Watching my father watch the dolphins, I felt like we were at an auction, bidding on the same item. It was an ugly, miserly feeling.

I couldn't sleep on Christmas Eve. Carrie and I shared my old bedroom, which now held a pair of single beds separated by my old tricolor nightstand. All the old anxieties were coming back, the deadness of a dark room, the stone-on-stone sound of a crypt top sliding closed as soon as I began drifting to sleep.

I heard Carrie stir during the night. "I can't sleep," I said.

"Keep practicing," she said groggily. "Practice makes practice."

"I was wondering why you quit writing. You had more talent than all of us. You always made it look so easy."

She exhaled through her nose and moved to face me. I could just barely see her eyes in the dark. "Let's pretend," she said.

I waited for her to finish. When she didn't I said, "Let's pretend what?"

"Let's pretend two people are lying next to each other in a room. Let's pretend they're talking about one thing and then another. It got too hard to put words in their mouths. They stopped cooperating." She rolled over, knocked her knee against the wall. "They started saying things like, I'm hungry, I'm thirsty, I need air. I'm tired of being depicted. I want to live."

I thought about her burn-ward story, the way boys were on one side of the room and girls were on the other. Before lights-out the nurse came in and made everyone sing and then closed a curtain to separate the boys from the girls. After a while I said, "You sleeping?" She didn't answer so I went downstairs.

I poured a glass of water, and looked around my father's office for something to read. On his desk were a dictionary, a thesaurus, and something called *The Yellow Emperor's Classic of Internal Medicine*, which I flipped through. *When a man grows old his bones become dry and brittle like straw and his eyes bulge and sag.* I opened the top drawer of his filing cabinet and searched through a stack of photocopied stories until I found a stapled manuscript titled "Mexico Story." I sat down on his loveseat and read it.

In Mexico, it began, *some men still remember Pancho Villa*. I prepared for a thinly veiled account of my father's and Lara's vacation, but the story, it turned out, followed a man, his wife, and their son on vacation in Mexico City. They've traveled there because the mother is sick and their last hope is a healer rumored to help even the most hopeless cases. The family waits in the healer's sitting room for their appoint-ment. The son, hiding under the headphones of his new walkman, just wants to go home. The mother tries to talk to him but he just keeps saying *Huh? Huh?*

The three of us go into a dim room, where the healer asks my mother what's wrong, what her doctors said, why has she come. Then he shakes his head and apologizes. "Very bad," he says. He tells a rambling story about Pancho Villa, which none of us listens to, then reaches into a drawer and pulls out a wooden back-scratcher. He runs it up and down along my mother's spine.

"How's that feel?" he asks.

"Okay," the mother says. "Is it doing anything?"

"Not a thing. But it feels good, yes? It's yours to keep, no charge."

I must have fallen asleep while reading, because at some point the threads came loose in the story and mother, father, and son leave Mexico for a beach that looks a lot like the one near our house. Hotels looming over the sea oats. The inlet lighthouse just visible in the distance. I sit on a blanket next to my father while my mother stands in knee-deep water with her back to us.

"She's sick," my father says. "She doesn't want me to say anything, but you're old enough to know. She's really... sick."

If she's sick she shouldn't be in the water, I think. Her pants are wet to the waist and if she wades in any deeper her shirt will be soaked, too. I pick up a handful of sand and let it fall through my fingers.

"So it's like a battle," he's saying. "Good versus bad. As long as we stick together, we'll get through it okay."

My mother walks out of the water. She is bathed in light and already I can barely see her. She sits next to us, puts her hand on my head, and, in the dream, I realize this is one of those moments I need to prolong. I put my hand over hers and hold it there. I push down on her hand until it hurts and I keep pushing.

"You can let go," she says. "I'm not going anywhere."

The next morning I found my father in checked pajamas near the Christmas tree. He carefully stepped over a stack of presents onto the tree skirt and picked up a gift from Carrie and me. He shook it and listened. He tapped on it with his finger.

"It's not a watch," I said.

He turned to me and smiled. "I've narrowed it down to two possibilities," he said. "Here." He waved me over. "Sit down, I've got something for you."

I sat on the couch and he handed me a long, flat package wrapped in red-and-white paper. "Wait, wait," he said when I started to unwrap it. "Guess what it is first."

I looked at it. All that came to mind was a pair of chopsticks.

"Listen," he said, taking it from me. He held it up to my ear and shook it. "Don't think, just listen. What's that sound like to you?"

I didn't hear anything. "I don't hear anything," I said.

He continued shaking the gift. "It's trying to tell you what it is. Hear it?"

I waited for it, I listened. "No."

He tapped the package against my head. "Listen harder," he said.

BAD KARMA

by ETGAR KERET

"Fifteen shekels a month can guarantee your daughter one hundred thousand in the event of your death. Do you know what a difference one hundred thousand can make to an orphan? It's exactly the difference between life as a lawyer and life as a receptionist in a dentist's office."

SINCE THE ACCIDENT, OSHRI had been selling policies like crazy. It wasn't clear whether this had anything to do with his slight limp or with the paralysis in his right arm, but people who'd sit through an appointment with him would take it all in and buy everything he had to offer: life insurance, loss of earning power, complementary health insurance, you name it. At first, Oshri kept recycling the same stories he'd used before—the one about the Yemenite who was run over by an ice-cream truck the very day he bought his policy, on his way to pick up his daughter from kindergarten, or the one about the guy from the suburbs who'd laughed when Oshri had offered him health insurance, only to call Oshri in tears a month later, having just received a diagnosis of pancreatic cancer. But very soon Oshri realized that his own personal story did the trick better than any of the others. There he was, Oshri Sivan, insurance agent, in the middle of a meeting with a potential client at a café near the Downtown Shopping Arcade, when all of a sudden, right in the middle of their conversation, a young man who'd decided to end his life jumps out of an eleventh-floor window in the building next to them, and *wham!* falls right on Oshri's head. The fall kills the young man, and our Oshri, who has just finished telling his Yemenite-and-ice-cream-truck story to another reluctant client, loses consciousness on the spot. He doesn't come to when they splash water over

 his face, or in the ambulance, or in the emergency room, and not even in the ICU. He's in a coma. The doctors say it's touch and go. His wife sits by his bed and cries and cries, and so does his little girl. Nothing changes for six weeks, until all of a sudden a great miracle occurs: Oshri comes out of his coma as if nothing had happened. He simply opens his eyes and gets up. And along with this miracle comes a bitter truth: our Oshri, who was so admirable in the things he preached, could kick himself for the way he practiced them, and since he'd never had a single insurance policy himself, he couldn't keep up with his mortgage. He had to sell his apartment and move into a rental. "Look at me," Oshri would say, wrapping up his sad story with a lame attempt to move his right arm. "Look at me, sitting here with you at this café, spitting blood to sell you a policy. If only I'd put aside thirty shekels a month. Thirty shekels, which is nothing really, barely a matinee ticket—without the popcorn—and I'd be lying back like a king, with two hundred grand in my account. Me, I had my chance and I blew it, but you—aren't you going to learn from my mistake, Motti? Sign on the dotted line and get it over with. Who knows what could land on your head five minutes from now." And this Motti or Yigal or Mickey sitting across from him would stare for a minute and then take the pen he held out to them with his good arm and sign. Every single one of them.

And so, without much effort, Oshri Sivan's battered bank account quickly began to recover, and within six months he and his wife had bought a new apartment with a much smaller mortgage than the one they'd had before. And with all the physiotherapy he got at the clinic, even his arm started getting better, though when clients held out their hands to him, he'd still pretend he couldn't really move it at all.

"There's blue and yellow and white and a soft sweet taste in my mouth. There's something hovering high above me. Something good, and I'm heading toward it. Heading toward it."

At night he went on dreaming about it. Not about the accident—about the coma. It was strange, but even though a long time had passed since then, he could still remember, down to the last detail, everything he'd felt during those six weeks. He remembered the colors and the tastes and the fresh air chilling his face. He remembered the absence of memory, the sense of existing without a name and without a history, in the present. Six whole weeks of present, during which the only thing he felt within him that wasn't the present was this little hint of a future, in the form of an unaccountable optimism attached to a strange sense of being. He didn't know what his own name was during those six weeks, or that he was married, or that he had a little girl. He didn't know he'd had an accident or that he was in the hospital, fighting for his life. He didn't know anything except that he was alive. And this fact alone filled him with enormous happiness. All in all, the experience of thinking and feeling within that nothingness was more intense and genuine than anything that had ever happened to him before. As if all the background noises had disappeared and the only sound left was true and pure and beautiful to the point of tears. He didn't discuss it with his wife or any other human being. You're not supposed to get that much joy out of being close to death. You're not supposed to get a thrill from your coma while your wife and daughter are crying their hearts out at your bedside. So when they asked whether he remembered anything about it, he said he didn't, he didn't remember a thing. When he woke up, his wife asked if, when he'd been in the coma, he'd been able to hear her and Meital, their daughter, talking to him, and he told her that even if he couldn't remember hearing them he was sure it had fortified him, and given him strength, on an unconscious level, and a desire to live. That was what he told her, but it wasn't true—when he'd been in the coma he really had heard voices on the outside sometimes. Strange, sharp, yet at the same time unclear, like sounds you hear when you're underwater. And he didn't like it at all. Those voices sounded menacing to him; they hinted at something beyond the pleasant, colorful now in which he was living.

"May you never know sadness again."

Ever since the accident, he and his wife made love a lot less often. They never talked about it, but he had the feeling that she thought it was okay. As if after the accident and everything she was so glad to have him back that she didn't need to keep score. Whenever they did make love it was nice, just as nice as it had been before, except that now his life had taken on another perspective, one that had to do with that world he'd been to, a world you can only reach when something falls on you from a high floor. It was a perspective that seemed to have dwarfed everything else. Not just the sex, but his love for her, too, and his love for his daughter—everything but the memory of it.

Oshri hadn't been able to make it during the shiva week to pay a condolence call on the family of the guy who'd dropped on his head. He couldn't make it to the unveiling of the headstone either. But when the first anniversary rolled around, he did go, with flowers and everything. At the cemetery there were only the guy's parents and his sister and some fat high school friend who looked to Oshri a little gay. They didn't know who he was. The mother thought he was her son's boss, since his name was Oshri, too. The sister and the fat guy thought he was a friend of the parents. But after everyone had finished placing little stones on the grave and the mother started asking around, he explained that he was the one that Nattie—that was the guy's name—had landed on when he'd jumped out the window. As soon as the mother heard this she began to cry, and started saying how sorry she was, and couldn't stop crying. The father tried to calm her down while giving Oshri suspicious looks. After five minutes of her hysterical sobbing, the father told Oshri stiffly how sorry he was for everything that had happened to him and that he was sure that Nattie, too, if he were still alive, would be sorry, but that now it would be better for everyone if Oshri left. Oshri agreed at once and quickly began to explain that he was almost fine by now and that when all was said and done it hadn't been so terrible—certainly not when you compared it to what Nattie's parents had been through—but the father cut him short in mid-sentence. "Are you planning to sue us?" he asked. "Because if you are, you're wasting your time. Ziva and I haven't got a penny to our names, you hear me? Not a penny." This only made the mother cry harder. Oshri mumbled something that was meant to reassure them, and left.

As he was putting his cardboard yarmulke back in the wooden box at the entrance to the cemetery, though, Nattie's sister caught up with him and apologized for her father. She didn't exactly apologize, actually, just said that he was an idiot and that Nattie had always hated him. This father, it turned out, had always been sure everyone was out to get him and in the end he'd been proven right by his business partner, who ran off with his money. "If Nattie could see how things here turned out, he'd be happy," the sister said, and introduced herself by name. Her name was Maayan. Out of habit, Oshri didn't take the hand she held out to him. After pretending so many times with clients that his arm was utterly paralyzed, it had reached the point where even when he was home alone he sometimes forgot to use it. When Maayan saw that he wasn't taking her outstretched hand, she shifted the handshake ever so naturally and touched him on his shoulder—a touch that, it turned out, made both of them a little uneasy. "It's strange having you here," she said, after they had both been silent for a moment. "What is Nattie to you? You didn't even know him, after all." "It's a shame," Oshri mumbled. "That I didn't know him, I mean. He sounds like somebody who was definitely worth knowing." Oshri wanted to tell her that his coming there wasn't strange at all. That he and her brother had some unfinished business between them. There had been so many people at the café that day, and of all the people there, he'd been the one that Nattie had fallen on. But he knew this would sound stupid, so he asked instead why Nattie had killed himself—so young and all. Maayan shrugged drily. He wasn't the first person to ask her that, Oshri guessed, and she

hadn't really had an answer for the others either. Before they went
their separate ways, he gave her his business card and said that if
she needed any help, no matter what it was, she
should call. And she smiled and thanked him but
said she was an independent person and managed
very well on her own. After taking another look
at the card, she said, "You're an insurance agent?

That's really strange. Nattie always hated insurance—he said it was
bad karma. That taking out a policy was like the opposite of believ-
ing things would go well." Lots of young people think that way,
Oshri said, but once you have children you look at things differently. And even if you want to believe things will go well, you can
never be too careful. And she smiled and nodded. They both knew
she wouldn't be calling.

While Oshri was on his way home from the cemetery, his wife
phoned. She wanted him to pick up Meital from the class she took
after school, and Oshri agreed right away, and when she asked him
where he was, he lied and said he'd had an appointment with a client in Netanya. He couldn't explain to himself just why he'd lied. It
wasn't because of the touch that he could still feel on his shoulder,
and it wasn't because he'd gone to the memorial service for no good
reason. If anything, it was because he was afraid she'd get a sense of
how grateful he was to that guy, Nattie, for deciding to put an end
to himself.

"Pleasant dreams."

When he was awake he couldn't remember exactly what that world
of the coma had felt like, and he probably couldn't have described
it if he'd tried. Only once had he made the effort, with a blind

woman to whom he'd been trying to sell life insurance. He wasn't sure why he'd expected her, of all people, to understand, but after three sentences he realized he was only scaring her, so he stopped. In his dreams, though, he really could go back there. And ever since that day in the cemetery, his coma dreams recurred more often. Sometimes more than once a night. And ever so slowly he felt himself becoming addicted to them. So much so that in the evenings, long before he got into bed, he would begin to tremble with excitement, like someone who after many years in exile was getting on the flight that would take him home. It's funny, but sometimes he was so excited that he couldn't fall asleep. And then he'd find himself lying in bed, frozen, beside his sleeping wife, trying to lull himself to sleep in all sorts of ways. One of them was masturbation. And ever since that memorial service, whenever he masturbated, he'd think of Maayan, and how she'd touched him on his shoulder. It wasn't because she was beautiful. And it wasn't that she wasn't beautiful, though her beauty was the fragile kind that comes with youth. The kind whose expiration date was coming up very very soon. As it happened, his wife had once had that same kind of beauty, many years ago, when they first met. But that wasn't the reason he would think of Maayan. It was because of the connection between her and the man who had helped him reach that world of colors and quiet, and when he'd masturbate over Maayan, it was as if he was masturbating over a world that suddenly, thanks to her, had taken on a woman's shape.

Meanwhile, he was churning out policies at a dizzying pace. Without even meaning to, he got better and better. Now, when he tried to sell them, he'd often find himself in tears. It wasn't a manipulation. It was real crying that came out of nowhere. And it would shorten the meetings. Oshri would cry and then he'd apologize, and right away the clients would say it was okay and sign. It made him feel a little like a swindler, the crying, though it was as genuine as could be. And because of it, he could also work fewer hours, which allowed him to sleep later. On weekends he could spend sixteen or twenty hours sleeping, until it reached the point where his wife asked him to go to the doctor for a checkup. And Oshri went, because he didn't want his wife to suspect anything, and when he told the doctor about all the hours he spent sleeping he tried to seem unhappy about it. The tests showed nothing. The doctor recommended more sports and all kinds of changes in his diet. Oshri promised he'd try, and later gave his wife some half-false version of the visit that suggested that sleeping a lot was part of the recovery process.

"Congestion on the coastal road"

One weekend when they were returning with their daughter from a visit to his wife's parents on a kibbutz, they passed an ambulance and a two-car collision. The drivers ahead of them slowed down to rubberneck. His wife said it was disgusting, that only in Israel did people behave that way. Their daughter, who'd been asleep in the back, woke up because of the sirens. She put her face up to the window in time to see one man, who was covered in blood, uncon- scious, being carried away on a stretcher. She asked them where they were taking him and Oshri told her they were taking him to a good place. A place filled with colors and tastes and smells that you couldn't even imagine. He told her about that place, about how your body becomes weightless there, and how even though you don't want anything, everything there comes true.

How there's no fear there, so that even if something is going to hurt, when it happens it turns into just another kind of feeling, a feeling that you're grateful to be able to have. He went on and on talking until he noticed his wife's chiding look. On the radio they reported heavy traffic on the highway, and when he looked in the rearview mirror again he could see Meital smiling and waving bye-bye at the man on the stretcher.

THE BEGINNING
OF A PLAN

by SHELLY ORIA

IN 1991, I WENT TO JAIL for canning goods without a license. My factory was super small, really a mom-and-pop shop, but when they caught me it made national news because they blamed the whole Bruchtussis epidemic on me. A reporter named Dolly P. investigated my operation with the kind of zeal most people demonstrate only when their children's lives are at risk. Dolly P. had no children, but she had ambition. She traced the first case to the same small town in Israel that manufactured most of my ingredients. For a while, every time a kid ate bad canned soup it was my fault; the mother would go on television and cry, My baby is coughing all the time now, my baby never used to cough, and the newswoman would wipe away a tear, sigh, and remind the public once again that my trial would soon begin. I got ten years.

I was a tough woman, a strong woman. But even the toughest

human being feels the sting of mortality when the law comes and says, Give us the best decade of your life. I'd just turned twenty-one; it hadn't even been a year since I'd left Israel. I had to escape.

Dolly P. was visiting me on a weekly basis, out of guilt. One day I told her, That's all very nice, but I need to get out of here, and what can you really do for me? She said, There's talk of a time-stop, you know, like in the Middle Ages—why don't we wait a few days, see what's what. I said, Dolly, what the hell are you talking about? If you don't want to help me out just say so. I knew how to work her. She said, What do you need? I said, A rope, a knife, a pickup truck. She said I do this for you and we're even, that's it. I said, I get out, we'll talk.

1991, PART 2

THE FIRST TIME-STOP
IN OVER A THOUSAND YEARS

The first thing people noticed when time stopped: clocks and watches. Nobody could bring back the ticking. Expert horologists from around the world were working the case day and night, except there was no day and no night, only a dim gray. With time went the date: calendars disappeared, the top-right corners of newspapers were naked, and the postmarks on letters just said SENT.

Time Counters started emerging everywhere. They would stand in public places and count out loud: seconds, minutes, hours. They were determined to prove that time hadn't really stopped, that this was only a problem of counting mechanisms, and that humans had to step in and do the work until things got better. It soon became apparent that no one could reliably count time for longer than ten hours, so Time Counters formed teams and used special signals to let each other know when one Counter wanted the next to get ready. They were extremely meticulous, but really they were nothing more than singers of repetitive numbers. After a while they began to fade away.

Dolly P.'s newspaper ran the story of my escape twice in a row, in successive dateless editions, then had me on the front page a third time, when it became clear that nobody was reading the paper anymore. For the first time in a long time I thought, Maybe I can find a way to feel safe. Most people I talked to assumed we all had no future, that we were trapped in that moment when time stopped, but I'd always say, We never had a future anyway, only our *assumption* that the future was coming. What's keeping you from assuming? I'd ask. Assume! I wouldn't say these things to upset people; I just never understood that point of view. On more than one occasion, I had a beverage thrown in my face.

AN INTERVAL
THE TIME-STOP STOPS

Eventually, it happens. A child sees a flower, maybe a lilac, or a rose, and insists that it has grown since he saw it last. He is young enough to hope.

The following day, a dog gives birth in some bathtub, to the amazement of her owners, who didn't realize she was pregnant. In a different place altogether, numbers appear on someone's pay stub: the date. Rumors start, and people grow optimistic, and with their optimism comes sundown, followed by sunrise the next morning. The last stubborn Time Counters faint on side roads, relieved of their duty, useless. For long days, beds are squeaking with hope, with anticipation, and a new generation of Clock Babies is conceived.

As can be expected, regaining a state of normalcy is not a thing that happens overnight. A good example: when time resumes, women who've been trapped in inactive pregnancies give birth within forty-eight hours, regardless of how far along they were when time stopped. The babies almost always survive, but life is never easy for them, with their transparent skin and unfinished features; people call them the half-baked, and generally consider them to be not completely human.

And yet somehow, in spite of the half-baked walking among us, in spite of mad, ersatz Time Counters who walk the streets of our cities mumbling numbers, convinced that time has not resumed, in spite of the various inedible, temporally corrupted fruits and vegetables that the earth keeps producing for at least a year, people forget. People forget because they choose to do so, and they choose to forget because

 remembering allows for the possibility of recurrence. People forget, and make cardamom tea, and fall in love, and buy ties. On Valentine's Day, they pay for overpriced dinners. Salmon in their mouth, they talk about their planned vacation for the summer.

At weddings, they try to guess who the next person to get married will be, and they smile at the thought of the entire family together in one place *again*, the joy it will bring. Every moment, they wait for the next. Every day, they think about the future. They forget.

I can say this: I never forgot. I found it curious that people around me did. I remembered, and I knew that time would stop again, only to resume again, only to stop again. It seemed obvious, like gravity, or death.

2001

PHIL

We met during the next time-stop, in 2001. By then I was a soaper; Phil came to see me in the Public Cafeteria, where I always held preliminary sessions with potential clients. These sessions were necessary because often people had very different ideas about the kind of service I was providing. After the first embarrassing misunderstanding, I decided that it was worth the time it'd take to go over the basics in advance: you will be cleaner than you've ever been in your life, but there will be no sexual activity of any kind, that sort of thing. Nowadays I charge for preliminary sessions, too, even though there's no actual soaping going on, but back then I had about ten regular clients and maybe six or seven here-and-theres, and I thought if I played too strict I wouldn't get any new ones. I was young. I didn't know yet that life usually worked the other way around.

At the cafeteria, Phil didn't do more than look at me and right away I knew where things were going. It seemed pointless to waste time, so I said, You remind me of someone—a man I had an affair with. I do? he asked. Yeah, I said, only his eyes were different and he was Israeli and my officer in the army. He smiled. Was the sex good? he asked. Phenomenal, I said. He liked this answer, which was a lie; the officer's philosophy was anything over four minutes was a waste of time. But men want to hear that sex can be phenomenal; it opens up possibilities.

I figured, it's a time-stop; people do all kinds of crazy things. Once the clocks start ticking again he'll remember that forbidden fruits aren't really worth eating and go back to his wife.

But it was my profession, not his wife, that brought up problems between us. Phil thought I shouldn't charge him anymore. I said, Then I can't soap you; it's against union rules. He said, That's just an excuse, you're not someone who'd let unions control her. Eventually I agreed, though I really needed the money, but our problems didn't stop. Clients were just showing up at my door whenever they needed a soaping, since setting up appointments during a time-stop is practically impossible. Phil would get crazy jealous every time I left him to tend to someone else. "Your hands all over his body" and all that bullshit. I said, If you want to be jealous at least be original about it. He said, Bambi, believe me, I'm as original as it gets.

Clocks were still at a halt when I came home one day to find him collecting his things, stuffing socks and shirts into brown paper bags.

 I felt every muscle in my body stiffen—I'd told him my real name, which was something I very rarely did in those days. The law people weren't after me anymore, but you can never be too careful. I stood there and looked at him for a while. Finally I said, Look, I'm a professional soaper. That's what I do. What did you expect? This isn't about that, he said. You miss your wife? I asked. I'm not going back to my wife, he said. I don't understand, I said. I thought you were the one, you know that? he said. But lately I'm not sure. I have to be sure, Bambi. You have to be sure? I said; I hoped that if I repeated it he'd realize how ridiculous he sounded. He looked right at me. This isn't working, he said.

For a while I stayed in bed, ignored the bell when clients rang it. Soon after, time resumed.

2011, PART 1
PHIL'S RETURN

All of a sudden, he came back.

Dolly P. had a colleague run a soaping piece centered on me. There was a picture and everything—me, gloves on, scrubbing a woman's arm with a toothbrush. Apparently, he saw it. At the door, Phil said, You haven't changed a bit. Time-stops will do that to you, I told him—I'm younger than I am. Actually, that's not accurate, Phil said—studies show that after time-stops cells grow quickly and the body makes up for lost time. Already we were arguing. And yet all I wanted to do was hug him; he was new and familiar and I realized how much I'd missed him.

I wanted to ask where he'd gone when he'd left ten years ago, where he'd been since, but I hate predictable questions. Instead, I offered watermelon. We could never share one when we were together, since fruits don't grow during time-stops; it was one of the only things I'd missed, in those days. It's my favorite fruit.

Phil and I sat on the floor and he popped the melon open. Red oozed all over the rug and for a second I wanted to suck it all in, like a vacuum cleaner, like a madwoman. But I didn't, because by then I was old enough to know that most people can't tell passion from weakness.

The next thing that happened was happiness. It crept up on me then, for a short while. Mornings he cooked eggs, and I didn't have to remind him how I liked them. Evenings we talked and talked, letting words linger and thoughts carry their weight. Maybe this is love, I thought: losing the need to rush somewhere else.

Then, two weeks in, I woke up one morning and thought, This doesn't feel right. He was snoring peacefully in my bed. I shook him and asked the inevitable question. He said he called the paper, got hold of Dolly P., paid her to give him my address.

I said, Dolly P. doesn't need money.

He said, I never said *how* I paid her.

I said, There's an agenda then, Phil. What's the agenda?

Sure took you long, darling, he said. I was waiting for you to ask.

This was Phil's idea: We create another time-stop. I thought he was being ridiculous and that's what I said. He said, Bambi, don't play with me. I said, Don't call me that if we're not really a couple; if you're only here to get results. I was getting dressed now. He was watching me with sex in his eyes, saying nice things about my body, but it takes more than that with me. I said, Phil, you stop this and you stop this right now. I'm leaving—four hours is what you've got. The apartment is yours, use anything, call anyone. Make a proposal, a presentation, a pitch. It's business now is what it is; you and I are done. When I'm back you get one shot. You talk, I listen, I make up my mind and that's it.

I hoped he would say Bambi, what do you mean we're done, forget this nonsense and come over here. Something like that. But he said okay. He seemed ready. I went to the park and sat on a bench. Four hours is a very long time when you feel cheated.

What this man put together in four hours was remarkable. The photographs were what really got me: me, all over my apartment, blown up to a size a woman should never see herself in. Me, huge, in prison; me, huge, in Ashdod, the Israeli town linked to the whole Bruchtussis fiasco; and the one that made me nauseated, me, even bigger, escaping. I said, How. That's all I could say, and I said it a few times. Phil was waiting, letting me take it all in.

Eventually he said, To save time, let's skip the bullshit. I know how you escaped from jail. I know everything, so let's not play here.

I hoped he was talking about Dolly P., about the pickup she got for me, the guard she bribed. But Phil's voice was telling a different story.

He said, It's maximum security, Bamb, the best in the country. You really think I'd buy the bribe story and stop looking? The bribe was only a decoy, right? I bet you didn't even need it. You just wanted the cops to find something when they came looking, right?

It was exactly right.

Did my feelings cloud my judgment? Sure. When you love a man it isn't some fanatical presentation that sways you; I was still hoping there was feeling at the bottom of things. But all in all I believe I had very little choice. This man had a map of my world.

Bambi, he said, I want you to do what you did in '91. I said, I can't, it's not something I control. He said Bullshit. I said Phil, it really isn't. It's a power that comes over me, that came over me then, not something I can summon. He said, You sure "summoned" it when you wanted your freedom back. The word *summoned* came out sarcastic and mean; meaner, I thought, than he'd intended.

I wanted him to understand. I said Phil, please listen now. One day in jail I got this sensation. It wasn't new, it's been coming and going since I was very young, but I never knew what to do with it. It always starts with this slow internal tremble, and then my brain begins to feel like copper, and I know that if I tilt it to one side and concentrate it can float, it can do things. That day in prison, I couldn't stop thinking about my cat. I had a cat then, Keyvan, and every time I closed my eyes I would see Keyvan passed out, or trying to drink water from the toilet to stay alive. I needed to get to him. Then I talked to Dolly P. The bribe was like you said, but the rest of the stuff was back-up—I didn't know what would actually happen. And then when it did happen, it was as mundane as buying tomatoes. I tilted my head, and everything froze—the world froze. It was almost disappointing, how easy it was; the opposite of magic. But Phil—once I was out, people were moving again, and my brain just felt like a normal brain. And I've never had that sensation since. All right? Do you understand?

He was quiet the whole time I talked, listening intently. Then he said, You simply let it go once you were out. It was a choice. I said, Maybe, but it didn't feel that way. He said, For our purposes, it doesn't even matter—you let it go, it let go of you, whatever.

Time had already stopped. You may have started something, but the world had the last say.

Phil's features softened, suddenly. He took my hand, and I let him. Bambi, he said, you're so naive. What about 2001, I asked—did I do that too? Phil smiled. It took me quite a while to figure that out, he said. But it doesn't matter now. You can stop time, Bambi, that's the important thing. And you're going to do it again for me.

We spent the next few days discussing the plan. The first thing I wanted to know was why, why he wanted this, and Phil talked about "doing it right this time." There are opportunities, great fiscal opportunities in a time-stop, he said, and we were stupid then, in 2001, just staying in bed and having sex. He said "having sex" like 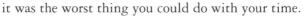 it was the worst thing you could do with your time.

Once time stops, Phil said, waiting as much as possible is key. People grow so desperate that they forget how to hope, he said. They forget how passing time feels, and then there's so much more we can do for them. He talked about banking all the energy that the world saves, and the ways in which we could capitalize on that energy. Time capsules were one. Selling dreams was another. He was excited. It seemed like I wasn't getting the whole story, but I didn't know what part was missing.

AN INTERVAL
1982, A MEMORY

There is a moment I remember well. I was twelve years old, discovering for the first time that desire made the air thinner. I was running in a field. This was in Israel, a field on the outskirts of the town where

I grew up. It was wartime, but the kind of war not too many people cared about. Also in the field: boys and girls I went to school with, a bonfire. My clothes were all stripes: gray and black, a matching skirt and top I had gotten the day before. This is what I heard: a boy I loved, who had dumped me a few weeks earlier, was now crazy jealous because I had a new boyfriend, a decoy boyfriend, a boy I never wanted. The two of them were trying to figure out who had the moral obligation to step back. Other boys were there to supervise, make sure things didn't escalate to a fight. This is what I learned: boys think that life is a call they get to make. This is why I started running: overturning this boy's rejection made me feel too powerful, like life was a call I got to make. The smoke in the air from the bonfire got in my lungs, and I thought I would run forever.

2011, PART 2
HOPE

I tried many times and nothing happened, but Phil never worried. He believed it was only a question of time, that I'd get it eventually. He said rumors in the street had already started, which showed that my brain was releasing some kind of substance, just like in '91. More than anything, he wanted me to believe in my power.

Every few days I'd try again, and fail again. It was clear what the problem was—there was nothing at stake. I knew that hurt Phil's feelings, because it showed him his goals were not my goals, that I hadn't really internalized this dream of his. But he never complained. He had enough patience and confidence for both of us.

What happens when you don't complain is that solutions find you. On a Tuesday morning, after we'd made love, Phil lay next to me and said Bambi, just relax now, can you do that for me? I said nothing but he knew I meant yes. He did all kinds of things with his fingers then; nothing too sexual, just tapping, touching without touching. He said, Close your eyes, and when I did it felt like I had a blanket. This went on for a while. Then he said, How about we do this, and when it's over we make a baby.

I never knew that this was what I wanted. But now I knew, and all of a sudden it was the only thing. My breathing hastened. That's right, he said. What do you say?

I had to ask now. What about your wife, I said. Long gone, he said, and then again, Long gone, and the way he said it answered the question I hadn't asked. I knew at that moment that our first encounter had not been random; knew that he'd already had intentions back then, the beginning of a plan. Whoever he'd been with before me had probably become unnecessary to its success. I knew all that, but I didn't care. There was no effort left in me, except the kind that makes you get up in the morning to braid a child's hair, write a note for school.

The next day time stopped again. I still experienced it as two entirely disparate events, in two different sites—my brain being one, the world another. But by now I knew better. Phil was the happiest I'd ever seen him. He couldn't stop talking. In our apartment, enthusiasm was everywhere, and in many ways we weren't part of the world anymore; outside, people were developing all the regular time-stop symptoms, reenacting patterns of behavior that were long ago declared detrimental, against studies and cold data, against the soft whisper of their own inner voice. At airports, riots were erupting. Airline company reps, or even the pilots themselves, would try to reason with the crowds; there was obviously no way to ensure safe travel, no way to synchronize sky traffic, and you'd think that people would understand that. Instead, they threw stones and broke glass and shouted things like "But I need to get to my convention, asshole."

On street corners, huge piles of microwaves accumulated; their frustrated owners unwilling to remember that at some point time would resume, that when others stepped back into their own kitchens and turned on cooking timers—casually, as if they'd always been able to do so—they, the people who were quick to discard, quick to give up hope, would form the famous ten-mile lines outside the various Baking Solutions stores.

This is the truth: there is no objective reason for time-stops to be as devastating as they are. For example: food can be tricky, sure, but no more people die of starvation during time-stops than at any other time (supplies always last until the manufacturing of Synthetic Food is in full force, and generally people are a lot less hungry). And not being able to travel by plane is limiting, yes, but in fact the difficulty of going anywhere else allows you to more fully be where you are. Really, the worst thing about time-stops is that they make people believe that time is something like oxygen.

Phil and I were working around the clock, so to speak. I followed every instruction he gave me. Together, we built a big device that looked like a satellite dish, and another one that Phil called the Medusa—a big silver ring with eight arms like hooks. Both fit in what used to be my study, after we took everything else out. The satellite dish, facing the window, was meant to receive much of the energy saved by the time-stop (up to 70 percent of it, Phil said proudly), and the Medusa was to store that energy and later convert it into a blue, greasy liquid that Phil would use to make his products—

mainly pills (those known today as T. pills) and these oddly shaped metal discs that allow some people to relive scenes from their old lives. (I personally see nothing but gray snow on my screen every time, which has been the subject of quite a few clashes between us—Phil believes that I'm blocking the feed on purpose somehow.)

We worked together, but it never felt that way; often I would shout out to Phil only to discover he was standing right next to me. I asked as little as possible about it all, afraid of the information as if it were another person lurking around the house. It was clear—this was Phil's main course, the one he'd been waiting for his entire life. I think he assumed I would come around eventually. I was waiting for him to be full, and trying not to resent him for his undying hunger. Waiting, when time is standing still, is not an experience I wish on anyone with a beating heart.

I used to be different; I used to find comfort in time-stops. I'd close my eyes and feel like I was in some underground maze— I couldn't get anywhere, but I wasn't supposed to. I try to remind myself of that every time I open my eyes to a new gray day. Still, I often forget.

This all happened a long time ago, though experts would argue that I can't technically say that. That's what it feels like, anyway, and I am now part of the Time Language Movement, so using these terms is a cause I spend my days fighting for. We believe in the power of language, and we believe that by using time-expressions we can, at the very least, create a reality in which the illusion of passing time is so strong that it substitutes for the functions of the real thing in essentially every way.

Nobody in the movement knows about Phil, or about my

involvement in what is now referred to as The Big One. I believe that since we're all working for the same cause, none of that should matter. Phil, in turn, believes we're no different from Time Counters and other types of weirdos.

These days he mainly operates from what he calls the Factory—a huge facility just outside of town, where they used to make cribs before everyone stopped needing to buy new ones. I know where it is, but I've never been there. If things between us were different, if I woke up one day and believed in his operation and wanted to do my part, I imagine he would take me over, give me the grand tour. I imagine he'd want me to fully understand the mechanics behind the dam that holds time back. I imagine he'd be happy. But I can't do it, and faking is never an option with Phil.

I still practice my profession, in order to spend as much time away from home as I can. I rent a small bath at a Soaping Inc. downtown. They call me every time one of my clients shows up, and I usually drop everything and go. It's a good arrangement for me, given that I can't see clients at home anymore; letting strangers into the apartment is exactly the kind of mistake Phil would never make. If anyone ever knew enough to come looking, the files stacked in his study (once mine, then ours, now his) would expose everything. It sometimes seems that when I so much as look at them in passing, he can sense it.

There's no phone at the Factory, no way to reach Phil when he's there, and yet every morning before he leaves he says, I'll be at the Factory, as if we're already a family, a normal one, and maybe our daughter would have an earache and I would need him to come home.

Yesterday, we were sitting on the balcony, drinking champagne and eating crackers. The dim gray light outside was getting to me, the way it often does. I looked at the color of the champagne in my glass, then at the gray light, and again, and again. I was trying to concentrate so that one would somehow spark the other, but whatever gift I had, it's gone; I sold it for hope.

Phil said, Bambi, that's cute what you're trying to do. He was mocking me, and it hurt, of course, but I've gotten used to that sort of pain. I looked at him. Sometimes he says unkind things but you can still see kindness underneath them. At the end of each evening, before we go to sleep, he goes to the kitchen and checks my vitamin jar, to make sure I've taken all my Nutrient Pills for the day. I said, What about what you promised me, Phil? What about the baby? I'd intended never to ask him that, but all of a sudden I forgot why.

He said, We'll get there, Bamb, we'll get there. When? I asked. How about next year? he said—2012? Pretending to set a date was his favorite joke these days.

I decided to try a different approach. Phil, I said, look at us. We have all the money in the world. Isn't that enough? It's enough, Phil, don't you see that?

I assumed that he'd feign agreement, let me relax; we both knew that he wasn't just making a profit, but also holding on as tight as he could, sitting on top of the whole still world without leaving our balcony. But he just sat there with a smile on his face that I'd never seen before, and seemed immersed in some conversation I couldn't hear. Finally he got up, put the champagne glass down, helped a few crumbs slide down his pants. He looked down at me, and sternness took over the smile. I never understood women, he said. So smart and so stupid at the same time. I was waiting for him to explain, and then realized that he wouldn't, because he wasn't talking to me, not really. He was quiet for a few seconds, then said, Money? Money? For fuck's sake, Bambi, we're living here in your crummy little apartment and you still think it's about the money?

He took a deep breath that said my stupidity caused him great pain. His disappointment hung heavy in the air, and I knew this was the moment Phil had given up on me for good. I wanted to drink all the champagne until it made me throw up, then drink some more. Money, Bambi, he said like he was the president of a great nation and I was the ignorant masses he was preaching to, is always, always, a means to an end. Remember that if you remember nothing else. And with that he turned his back to me and walked into the living room. I noticed there were crumbs on his ass that he must not have been aware of, remnants of the crackers we'd eaten. This would have bothered him, I thought. Phil is a very tidy man.

PINECONE

by MICHAEL CERA

CARROLL SILVER ONCE CONSIDERED himself hot property. Yep, he used to think to himself, I exude all sorts of delicious mystery. Girls look at me and they think Holy hell what I wouldn't give to have that man kiss me on the neck. Men and boys alike look at me and think to themselves What am I? What the hell kind of scum am I? I thought I was good, but just look at that fellow. Look at him. Where on earth does somebody like that come from? Where can I get those clothes? Approximately how long will it take me to transform myself to at least look like somebody who has enough sense to admire and try to emulate someone like him?

Carroll no longer considered himself hot property.

In the morning, Carroll would glance at the mirror only to find his horrified reflection staring back at him. He'd furrow his brow and tense his face up skeptically, in disbelief at what he was seeing. He'd slap the skin under his chin and grab a fistful of it, tugging on it with breathy contempt. He'd run his fingers through his hair, which had stopped growing around his ears the way it used to. In what seemed like a moment he had turned thirty-eight, become lonely, looked sloppy, and was hungry.

After several years of moderate success, Carroll was starting to become disappointed with the roles that he was being sent out for. Whereas he used to play the younger, more handsome brother, or perhaps a handsome only child, he was now being brought in for the annoying best friend, or the free-spirited uncle. One day while learning his lines in his trailer, Carroll made a frustrated phone call to his agent, which ended in him firing his agent, which led to him looking for a new agent, which led to him not being able to get a new agent. In an attempt to take his mind off of the severity of the matter, he stopped looking for an agent altogether and began going to bed early.

One evening, in the warmth of September, Carroll said enough of this and set out to get dinner. Tonight, healthy food, followed by an intense cardio workout. A salad, followed by a workout. A cheap salad. Need to start saving money. At least until I get a job.

Carroll's last job—the one that led to his firing his former agent—had now been eight months ago. He had been cast as a gym teacher in a comedy about a young basketball team. One day the prop master, Glen, asked him if he had a prefer-ence of pitch for the whistle he would be using in the role of Coach Kelman. He told him he didn't give a damn, he would just try to hit his mark, say the right lines, and otherwise keep quiet. The prop master laughed. He liked Carroll. Carroll hadn't meant to make him laugh and he certainly didn't like him back. In fact, he could hardly stand the prop master's laugh, and how red his face got when he was smiling. He was the kind of guy that Carroll, in his younger years, would have had a lot of fun with. Carroll was no longer in his younger years and the prop master made his skin crawl on a daily basis. Just hand me the fucking whistle and hand me the fucking clipboard, he thought to himself, and nobody is going to give a shit about the pitch of the whistle and nobody is going give a shit about what I have written on the forms that are clipped into my clipboard and nobody is going to even watch this stupid fucking movie except for little kids and everything's going to be fine.

He very much liked Sandra, the on-set wardrobe assistant. He liked her so much, in fact, that he folded and hung up his wardrobe in his trailer at the end of the day. In fact, he liked her so much that he wished on a daily basis that he didn't have to wear that stupid whistle and those gym shorts and the baseball cap when he was around her.

One morning, he stepped into his trailer and found a note from Sandra sitting on the bed. He smiled uncontrollably and locked his door. He giddily picked up the note, which read: *Hi hun yesterday during the bleachers scene your balls were showing when you were sitting down so I gave you a pair of black undies for today just so it won't happen again. I'll put them in with your wardrobe from now on.*

Carroll was walking down the hall of his apartment building, on his way to get himself a salad before his huge cardio workout, when he ran into his neighbor. His neighbor was a twenty-year-old kid with short blond hair and blue eyes whom Carroll saw constantly. He had no idea what this kid's name was, and it'd be too weird to ask, and he had a feeling the kid recognized him from movies, and that he'd want to exchange phone numbers if they exchanged names. So he kept their interactions brief as best he could.

He said Hey and the kid said Hey what's up? and he told him he was gonna grab something healthy for dinner and the kid said

Oh yeah what were you thinking? and Carroll said to the kid, who seemed to be in pretty good shape himself, that he didn't know, and did the kid recommend anything?

 Yeah, man, go to Fred's Chicken and get the chicken fingers with the famous sauce, they're unbelievable.

Hmm, Carroll thought. Sounds kinda junky. I should probably stay away from that.

At this point, the conversation had gone on much longer than Carroll ever could've anticipated. He tried to wrap it up.

Cool, he said. I'll head over there.

Hey, listen, if I give you some money, maybe could you grab me a Number One combo with double bread and no coleslaw and a sweet tea?

Sure, no problem.

I'll give you some cash when you come back.

Okay.

Damn, Carroll thought as he drove down Wilshire, headed to Fred's to make a food run for someone in better shape than he was whose name he didn't even know. So now I'm buying this fucking kid dinner? He'd better give me cash for this. I can't afford to be buying some punk's food for him just because I was decent enough to let him have his brief daily exchange with somebody he recognizes from movies. What I'll do is leave the food in the car, walk up to his place, collect the cash, and then say Oops I forgot your food in the car. And if in fact he doesn't have the cash, I'll say Oops then I don't have your food, shithead.

Damn, Carroll thought as he pulled up to the drive-thru window, I really shouldn't be eating this crap. When am I gonna start eating healthier?

Welcome to Fred's, can I help you?

Yeah hi there I'll have two Number One combos please. On the first one can you give me double bread and no coleslaw and on the second could I get no bread and no fries and a coleslaw with light dressing please?

Oh… my god, said the young, red-haired girl collecting cash at the first window. Aren't you Carroll Silver?

Yep.

She was cute, but what was the deal with her fingernails? As she grabbed the twenty from Carroll's hand, he couldn't help but notice her nails were scratchy little stubs. Jesus, he thought. Somebody close to her should really tell her how disgusting those things look.

Your movie *Thunder Clap* is my all-time favorite movie and I am not kidding it's my favorite movie ever!

Thank you very much.

Here's your change—I'm sorry for harassing you. She giggled.

Oh no, you're not harassing me at all.

John, this is Carroll Silver from *Thunder Clap*!

This fellow John then sauntered over to the window with a big stupid handsome grin on his face.

That is honestly the best movie, man. Can I shake your hand?

Sure.

The window closed for a minute. Carroll still had not been handed his food and was beginning to worry that they were intentionally trying to get him to stick around. He considered the fact that they may have been phoning some of their paparazzi friends and telling them to come quickly and that they would try to stall and keep him there as long as they could. The thought sickened him.

My chicken better not be getting cold back there.

Soon, all of the kids working there were on the other side of the window. Once again it opened. The original girl stood there with a boy.

This is Kevin, he loves *Thunder Clap* too, she said.

And *Pinecone* was a fantastic movie too, he added.

I didn't like *Pinecone*, the girl confessed.

Oh well, here, let me give you your money back then, Carroll said. Here you go, here's ten dollars. Did you have popcorn as well?

Um, yeah, she giggled. This was all very exciting.

Carroll planted another ten-dollar bill in her palm.

How about a beverage?

Yeah, I had a snack combo, she said.

Here you go, Carroll said as he removed yet another ten from his wallet and placed it in her open palm. Now you've got thirty of my dollars. Out of my pocket. Thirty dollars back for your ticket, popcorn, and beverage. My apologies for working so hard on something you didn't even like. Thank you so much for your honesty, now I can go back in time and not work so hard on that movie. I guess I'll just go back to the four months I spent learning American Sign Language and do something a bit more productive with my time. If only you getting your money back could undo the fact that you had to sit through it. I really wish it could. I do. The thought of you sitting there in that movie theater and looking at your watch every few minutes and wanting to go home to your comfortable living room just absolutely breaks my heart. No matter, now that you've got your thirty dollars back you can get yourself a manicure and disgust fewer customers with those utterly repugnant little suggestions of fingernails that are growing out of the ends of your hands and maybe someday you can even get a raise at this lovely little fast-food place you've gotten yourself hired at. One day, if you've got time, I'd love to hear the story of how you charmed your manager into hiring you. He must have seen deep into your soul that day, and seen something very special in you. I can only assume you had your hands plunged

deep into your pockets that day, or maybe this was before the plight
that is now your fingernails. Maybe back then they weren't quite so
decrepit and diseased. Say, is my chicken getting cold back there?

The young girl, stunned, closed the window and ran off with her
hands over her mouth, just as handsome John walked up with the
same moronic grin on his handsome face and a paper bag in hand.

Food's on us, Mr. Silver, he said as he handed Carroll the food.
Thanks for all the great movies.

When Carroll got back to his apartment building, the young
blond boy was hanging out in the hallway, waiting for him.

Awesome! the kid exclaimed. How much do I owe you?

Thirty dollars.

Son of a bitch what is the matter with me? She was completely cute.
And *Pinecone* was a disaster of a film, so why shouldn't she be honest
and come out with it? It was hard to watch. It was the result of an
absolutely retarded director wearing his hubris around his wrist and
making headstrong decisions regarding character development. You
would have thought it was directed by a nine-year-old. And so what if
she was unpresentable from the knuckles down? I'm
unpresentable from the knuckles up, for Christ's sake!
At least she'd never have the problem of having dirt
under her fingernails, with them being so unbecom-
ingly short. Hell if I could find a speck of dirt any-

where near them. I could have driven her home and told her all about
the film industry and how agents are bastards and casting directors
judge books by their covers and directors are obstinate and ruin scripts
with real potential, as did Jeff Koehler in the case of *Pinecone*, a script
that any actor of sound mind would've jumped through hoops to be
a part of! Talk about a damn shame. Goddamn that Jeff Koehler and

goddamn his headstrong decisions regarding character development. And excuse me, brilliant director, for making observations regarding the subtext of the character that *I'm* playing. Didn't realize "make your actors feel inadequate" was part of the job description. Maybe because it isn't. Pretty sure your job description is simply "direct the film and shut the fuck up." Piece of shit. Talk about a blunder. Anyway, that was a long time ago.

Hell with it, he thought. Like she was going to be my girl-friend or something? It'd be a marathon of embarrassment for the both of us. I could hardly take her to any events. As if I'm going to show up to the annual Critics' Choice luncheon with a girl that stands at a deep fryer all day biting her nails and daydreaming about famous people.

After pondering it for a short while in bed, where he had pulled up his shirt and was studying his stomach, Carroll decided that the main thing keeping him from exercising regularly was the lack of good music on his iPod. As soon as I get some great songs on that thing, he thought, I'll be going to the gym every afternoon and I'll be able to listen to songs I really love while doing a minimum half hour of cardio on the elliptical. And who knows, maybe I'll be like "When in Rome" and roll it into the full hour, as long as this thing's got another half hour's worth of awesome songs for me. And also probably I'll get really into it after the first week or so, once I start seeing my body getting better.

So off he went to Amoeba Records to rekindle his love affair with music, a love affair that had become dormant when he was a child. Around seven years old, Carroll had decided to give up his guitar lessons in order to focus on honing his acting powers.

He rubbed his hands together as he strolled through rows and rows of albums, each one a potential five pounds lost. Where to begin? he thought. I'm definitely going to be doing some muscle toning. Need to buy at least one heavy-metal album. Not too heavy though, I don't want my fellow gym-goer on the neighboring ellip tical to catch an earful of excess rock leaking from my earphones and become alarmed that they're working out next to a serial killer. Maybe some sort of Best of Heavy Metal compilation so that at least the odds are they'll recognize the songs and be able to associate me with some slight sense of familiarity. Though pretty soon they won't need the heavy metal to associate me with some slight sense of famil-iarity since I'm going to be at the gym every day probably roughly around the same time and they'll become familiar enough with me based on that alone. Maybe they'll even watch my development carefully and some day during the second week or so after they've noticed a transfor-mation they'll come up to me and say "Hey, keep it up, seems to be working for you." Maybe it'll be a woman. Maybe I'll say "Hey as long as you're here every day, ten men couldn't stop me from coming." And maybe she'll laugh and say "Well hopefully it won't come to that" and her fingernails will be long and healthy and shiny.

Carroll noticed that a silly-looking fellow, about ten feet tall with a goofy grin on his face, had sidled up beside him and was pretending to peruse the albums around him. They caught each other's eyes.

Hey, said the young man.

Carroll threw a head toss at him. Hey, he said. He pressed his lips together, donating a half smile that he'd hoped would signify the death of the exchange. He put his head down with finality and pretended to read the back of a Monster Ballads compilation CD.

Carroll Silver?

Carroll realized he'd been caught. Thrashing about the boat would only prolong the discomfort. Better, he thought, not to fight it. It'll all be over in a minute.

Yeah. Hi, how you doing? Carroll smiled and extended his hand.

 Can I get your autograph? said the man as he shook Carroll's hand, apparently not hearing what Carroll had said. He looked at him the way someone looks at a television. There he stood, gazing at him, mouth slightly open, a grin trying to emerge on his face.

Yeah, no problem. Do you have a pen or something?

The man looked down to search around in his pocket for a pen. As soon as he felt one, his head snapped back up to Carroll, as if Carroll would disappear if he didn't keep his eyes on him. He presented the pen, and a business card for Carroll to sign.

It's so weird seeing you here like this.

Yeah, it's pretty weird. Should I just put my name or did you want some kind of message or something?

Yeah, just write whatever you want. Could you make it out to Rex?

Sure thing, Rex.

Carroll looked around to see if they were attracting attention. Nobody seemed to notice them. He bit his lower lip and searched deep for something clever to write.

REX, KEEP YOUR EYES ON THE ROAD AND LOVE YOUR NEIGHBOR. ONLY ONE LIFE TO LIVE. CARROLL SILVER.

Wow, man! Thanks so much, my girlfriend is going to flip!

No problem, Rex. Have a good day, now.

Is Silver your real name?

No.

Yeah, I figured. I hear a lot of actors change their names to make them sound cooler.

I didn't change mine to make it sound cooler.

What's your real last name?

Sorry, Rex, but if I wanted you to know that, I wouldn't have changed my name.

Carroll had changed his name to make it sound cooler. His real last name was Hawbaker. Growing up as Carroll Hawbaker was not something he recalled with fondness. Some of the less clever kids in school used to call him Cockbaker. Carroll always thought this was stupid and lazy of them. It doesn't rhyme in the least, it isn't an actual vocation, and it doesn't imply that he's gay or dumb or any of the other things that malicious nicknames tend to imply, so why even bother calling him that? And why did it hurt so much? There's no such thing as a cockbaker. The whole conceit of it is ridiculous. Somebody that bakes cocks? Like human cocks? What on earth? Still, he didn't think twice about changing his name upon becoming a member of the Screen Actors Guild. Carroll Silver sounded much less clumsy and he figured having a cool last name like Silver might distract people from the fact that his first name is Carroll, a lady's name. In fact, while the kids in school were entertaining themselves by calling him Cockbaker, he breathed a sigh of relief that they didn't ever lock on to his having a girl's first name. Carroll had always hated his first name. Why Carroll? he always thought. That's a girl's name. I'm not a girl. I'm a guy. He deduced at an early age that he would mind being named Carroll far less if he were in fact a girl. One day in his adult life, while lying in bed thinking, he decided that he would also mind not having a lady in his life less if he were a girl.

Hey, do you think I could get a picture with you?

Sorry, Rex but I'd rather not do that right now. It's a bit embarrassing in here with people around and everything.

Ah come on please? My girlfriend would flip.

Hey, no means no, Rex. Now leave me alone, huh?

The young man walked off with a half grin still plastered on his face, looking down at his autographed business card with delight. Carroll muttered a few words under his breath about him being a reprobate and such, and pretended to look at some more albums. He left the store empty-handed, deciding that money was tight and he'd have to work out without music until he was more financially comfortable.

Money got tighter as time went by. Carroll was becoming increasingly aware of how few auditions he was being sent out for. He attributed this, in large part, to his not having an agent to make him aware of auditions. Carroll began to go through the newspaper looking for open casting calls. He went in for one and was brought into a room with four other actors. They stood in a line and were not required to do anything but stand there and let the producers look at them. He found this degrading and didn't put his heart into it. He figured the guy next to him would get the part since he was wearing a see-through mesh shirt and was very openly in good shape. What's the point if it's all a beauty contest? he thought.

It occurred to Carroll that selling a few things for some quick cash might not be a bad idea. He inspected his apartment for anything of value. The only thing he could find was his iPod, which he decided he could not sell because if he sold his iPod he would definitely never start working out. Carroll decided to sit and think. He was smart, after all. As far as he was concerned he had become smarter and smarter over the years. Surely he could think of a plan to turn things around. He was in a brief mire, that was all. He'd had worse troubles than this. Much worse. And as far as his loneliness, he was none too concerned. He was choosing to be lonely. If he lowered his standards even the slightest bit, he could probably be with any woman he wanted. If he had not been repulsed by the drive-thru girl's slatternly, disgusting excuses for fingernails he would've asked her out right then and there. He would've said, "Very glad you liked *Thunder Clap*, how would you like to come back to my apartment sometime and get a rare and unique insight into the life of an actor and where all the emotion and humanity come from? Then later perhaps we can have some lunch and you can run lines with me for the movie I'm working on next." If only those damn nails weren't so damn unsightly. She seemed sweet enough. Seemed to have a nice laugh, and definitely seemed playful. She was laughing and playful at first when he began to refund her money for the movie ticket and popcorn and beverage.

What have I done? he thought.

At Fred's Chicken the smell of ketchup packets and floor cleanser hung in the air. The red-haired girl was working behind the counter, biting her nails, as Carroll strolled in. She noticed him and quickly stopped, shooting her arm down by her side. She shrunk a bit, letting the air out of her shoulders, and looked sheepishly at the counter. Carroll made his approach.

How you doing? he said with a nod and a smile.

Fine sir how are you today? she said to the counter.

Oh, I'm pretty good. Chicken was so good I thought I'd come back and get some more of it.

That's good, sir.

Service was great too.

A cloud of tension hovered above their heads. The young girl was unable to make eye contact with Carroll. He sensed her suffering. He considered himself an expert in reading human emotions. He'd always assumed this was why his acting powers came so naturally to him.

Never got your name, by the way.

Oh. It's Molly.

Molly.

Molly now had her eyes locked on a specific button on the cash register. She felt safe there. With her gaze locked on this particular button, she bit her lower lip and raised her eyebrows. Carroll felt as though she'd been hurt in her life. As an actor, he had a good sense of "backstory." He imagined that people were repelled by her because of how poorly she maintained her fingernails. Still, she was a person. Carroll looked down at the floor.

Molly, he said. I just want to tell you I think you're about the most beautiful girl I've ever seen around here and I've seen my share. You've got a natural pulchritude that just radiates from you. You probably can't even help it. It's very natural. Your beauty is beyond your control. Not to mention your cheekbones. I know some girls who'd absolutely kill to have your cheekbones. They're completely graceful. As is the rest of you. I really just had to tell you that.

After a moment, he lifted his head.

Molly's eyes were little pools of bliss. She still had her lip tucked under her teeth, but her gaze had found its way to Carroll's eyes. The more she looked at him looking at her, the moister her eyes became, and pretty soon her lip trembled so much that it came loose from the grips of her upper teeth and she took a short little breath in through her mouth.

Thank you.

You're welcome. It's really the truth. There's something really wonderful about you, it's just so nice.

She exhaled with a laugh, and managed to speak between breaths.

Thank you, she said as she wiped her nose on her sleeve.

By any chance have you heard of the annual Critics' Choice luncheon?

No.

Oh, well, it's this thing they have every year where basically all of the top critics invite a handful of actors and filmmakers to have lunch somewhere fancy and everyone is allowed to bring a guest. I've been invited in the past and am expecting to be invited this year because I've gotten to know a lot of the critics very well over time. I was wondering if maybe you'd like to join me. It will be a delicious lunch, all paid for, and it will be wall-to-wall famous folks.

Molly had gotten her breathing under control and was now at a loss for words.

You want to bring me?

Nothing in the world could ever possibly make me happier.

I don't know what to say.

Well, Molly, think of it as an apology for the way I behaved the other day in the drive-thru. It was absolutely uncalled-for behavior, as well as groundless. My actions were puerile and my arguments were flat-footed. There are no winners in those kinds of fights. And also, you were only telling the truth about *Pinecone*. There's no law that says you had to like that movie. It's a free country, different people like different movies. Some people like that movie, and you and a lot of people don't like it. What it is is a textbook example of a script with mega potential being ruined by a tragically untalented filmmaker, that's all it really is.

Listen, Mr. Silver. I really don't want you to feel like you have to bring me to the luncheon just because you hurt my feelings. It was really nice of you to come in here in the first place. I don't want you to feel like you're doing me any favors.

Molly, it would be my absolute distinct pleasure to be able to show you a good time at the annual Critics' Choice luncheon. And my mother always told me if someone's trying to do something nice for you, you ought to let them.

Molly had no chance of fighting the smile that was crawling onto her face. She felt warm all through her body and her hands were scrunched up into little excited fists.

I would absolutely love to go with you!

Fantastic news! Why don't I go ahead and get your phone number.

 Molly could hardly stand still. She anxiously recited her phone number to Carroll as he wrote it down on a napkin, making him repeat it back to her to make sure he'd copied it correctly.

Great! he said.

I think I'll hire someone to do my hair that day! My friend Samantha did that for prom and she looked so pretty!

Sounds great, he said with a smile.

All right, well I really should get back to work or I'll get in trouble.

Of course, back to real life. Well, hope you have a great rest of the day.

You too! said Molly, brimming.

Carroll made for the door with a smile on his face. He had his hand on the handle when he paused, pivoted on his heel, and strolled back toward Molly.

Oh, you know, there's just one more thing, I think.

Molly looked up from a new plastic bag of Styrofoam cups that she was ripping into.

Oh, what?

Carroll sauntered over to the counter.

You know, it's just that since we're kind of starting fresh, it occurs to me that in terms of being comfortable with each other and everything and not having anything between us, I wonder if maybe it's just a little weird and tense to have that whole thirty-dollar thing between us.

Molly nodded her head, brow furrowed.

Oh yeah, I see what you mean.

Yeah, because things would probably just be better if there was absolutely nothing between us and we didn't have any kind of unresolved issues or anything like that.

Yeah, absolutely. Well, what do you think would be the best thing to do?

Carroll scratched his neck and scanned the ceiling with his eyes.

Yeah, I guess that's just what I'm trying to figure out—it's like, how do we kind of erase everything and wipe the slate clean?

Molly bit her lip and looked at the counter, deep in thought. Carroll also seemed to be wracking his brains. Suddenly, it hit him. He opened his mouth slightly, trying to decide whether or not to come out with it. He opened his eyes wide and rolled them to the left side of his head.

What? said young Molly, sensing that Carroll had had an epiphany.

Carroll paused.

Well, I mean the only thing I can think of is if you just give me the thirty dollars back and then it's like that whole thing just never even happened.

Molly's eyes brightened as an exhilarated smile came to her face.

Of course, that makes total sense!

Still smiling, Molly ran into her employee locker and fished the three tens that Carroll had given her a few days prior out of her purse. When she came back out, Carroll was studying the napkin with her phone number on it and repeating the number to himself. He smiled as she rounded the corner.

Here you go, silly, Molly said as she presented the money to Carroll.

Perfect! said Carroll. He grabbed the three bills and shoved them into his pocket. He wiped his hands for effect, and then extended one hand out to Molly.

Pleased to meet you, my name is Carroll Silver.

Pleased to meet you too! said Molly, as she shook Carroll's hand. My name is Molly, I'm a big fan.

If only all my fans could be so pretty.

Carroll and Molly smiled at one another. Carroll looked down at Molly's hand as he shook it, and then looked up again to meet her eyes, trying to hide his repulsion.

Well Molly, I'd better be headed out. Gonna skip the chicken for today, already got what I really came in here for.

Molly smiled and winked. Carroll headed for the door.

So I should be getting that invitation in the mail any day now. The luncheon is in March, so I'll give you a call some time in early March.

 Carroll climbed into his car. He buckled his seatbelt and put the key in the ignition. He looked at the napkin with Molly's phone number on it. He nodded his head and exhaled through his nostrils before crumpling the napkin into his glove compartment. He then took the thirty dollars out of his pocket and folded it into his wallet.

Carroll no longer considered himself hot property.

DIAMOND ACES

by CARSON MELL

M Y DAD ALWAYS LEFT around noon, and we usually ate dinner without him. When I was up late watching talk shows he'd sometimes come in smelling like pipe tobacco, even though I only saw him smoke cigarettes. I didn't know what he did for work.

I knew that before me and my brothers were born he managed a club called Diamond Aces. He didn't tell me about it himself, but there were plenty of his grizzled old friends around to do it for him—the ones that stayed outside during Christmas parties. "Lord, how I miss Diamond Aces!" they'd say, long drag off a cigarette, the only thing glowing back there in the shadows. Everything about these men was dingy. Even their eyes had lost their sheen.

From what I could cobble together from their stories, Diamond Aces was for a time the most popular strip club in all of Phoenix. It was so popular that women went there, too—guys took their wives. This was all pre–table dance, of course. One of these kooks even had a picture of the place in his back pocket. I've pretty much forgotten that photo now, but I remember painted coconuts, a couple of palm trees piped with neon. My dad wasn't in the picture.

He never really did retire. Dad hustled until the day he died. But around seventy, when I was twenty-eight and William IV had just been born, he got to the point where he was resting a couple of weeks in between his gigs. I still didn't know what he did.

The last time I ever saw him whole was when June and I brought the baby down to Tucson, to show off our boy to him and his new Brazilian wife. The kid wriggled and cried and the two wives clapped above the bed, tickled at the new William. Grandpa just hung back with his thumbs in his belt loops. Eventually he moseyed over, poked him in the stomach. "Cute one." Then he stepped away and the women folded back into place.

I was over on the love seat, watching all the family going on from a safe distance. I was just glad to be sitting.

"You want to go on a little road trip?" Dad asked me.

"When?"

"Right now. Just up to Tempe real quick. There's somebody there I'm supposed to meet."

"Sure," I said.

And the women, high on baby love, gave us permission so long as we were back by dinner.

On the way up there we smoked cigarettes with the windows down, wind roaring around. I pondered bringing up the troubles that June and I were having, love troubles, but decided against it.

"I ever tell you about Diamond Aces?" Dad asked over the wind.

"Some of your friends did."

"What'd they tell you?"

"That it was popular, that it was tropical. That it was a strip club."

"Not a strip club," he said. "It was exotic dancing. The girls wore coconut bras and skirts. Belts made out of bananas with glitter on the ends. Guys brought dates there."

"Yeah, they told me that."

The lighter popped out, Dad pushed it back in.

"The girls never took their tops off?" I asked him.

He could sense my disappointment. "Well," he put the word out slow with two lungfuls of smoke, "sometimes when the moon was full, Willy. Sometimes the bottoms came off."

We were going up to Tempe to meet with a "younger guy." Younger than my pop but older than me. Somewhere in between, somewhere in his forties. Dad took a scrap of paper out of his coat. "Phillip Gelante. P-h-i-l-l-i-p. Phillip Gelante."

He was standing out in front of his club when we pulled up. The place was called Cherries, just off of the 202. Built of cinder block with nothing in the planters. It used to be a doctor's office.

Either Phillip's face was too small or his head was too big. The features were all bunched up in the middle, like the moon man with a rocket in his eye, and his hair was puffed up so high that it lagged behind when he snapped his head around.

He shook my dad's hand with both of his. "Thank you so much for coming out, Mr. Churchfield, I really appreciate it."

"No problem, no problem at all. Having a little trouble with your club here?"

"Yeah, I just—something about it ain't working."

"Something's wrong with it," Dad said, surveying the plain tan building. A semi rumbled past and the ground shuddered. The sun was going down, pulling a hundred kinds of orange through the banded clouds.

"You know, my father took me to Diamond Aces when I was nineteen and I'll never forget it."

"You remember if there was a full moon that night?"

"No, no, I don't remember if there was." He was taking everything my pop said very seriously, desperate to juice every last drop of wisdom out of each new sentence.

Inside Cherries one big stage ran along the far wall. Another stuck out into the room like a giant ironing board, and there were brass poles in the centers of both. It took a minute for my eyes to adjust—the only light came from cracks in the black-painted windows and some low-watt colored bulbs. There was a row of grimy booths opposite the big stage where the girls could do lap dances. No customers, though, just two worn-out dancers in neon bikinis smoking cigarettes and staring out at the strange place they'd planted themselves.

Phillip led us into his office. The windowsill behind his desk was decorated with a collection of dried-out desert bugs, stones, and a piece of dog shit dipped in shellac and outfitted with a beak and googly eyes. It was labeled "Arizona Turd Bird."

"We open at noon, haven't had a customer yet. This is typical, it's... shit!" He spit the little word through his teeth, pounded his desk. "What do I do here, Will?"

My dad opened one hand, laid it out palm up. "You want bees, you get honey." He opened the other. "You want customers, you get beauty."

"I know that, Will."

"Really? Sure fooled me with those two Garfield girls you got perched out there." I think he meant they were lazy-eyed, but I'm not sure.

"Those are the daytime girls."

Dad nodded, took an intricately carved meer-schaum pipe from inside his coat and began to pack it. "Nighttime much better?" he mumbled past the stem.

"No."

He lit the pipe with a book of matches from Phil's desk, tossed them back. "Where're you advertising?"

"Everywhere you're supposed to. Sex shops, *New Times*. I even got a couple of guys putting up fliers around ASU. We have a five-hun-dred-dollar pot on amateur night and still, shit. Nada."

My dad stood, smoothed down his sport coat. "Well, let's check this place out."

We went back through the main room and into a short hallway. It led into a large concrete room with a drain in the middle of the floor and a bunch of cleaning supplies in one corner. There was something unnerving about the place, like you'd recognized it from a dream. Opposite the supplies was a man about my age playing a colorful game on a big, humming computer. He turned and looked at us.

"This is Reese," Phil said.

"R-e-e-s-e," my dad said.

We both shook his cold hand. He looked kind of deformed, same as Phil, same as everybody we met at Cherries that evening.

My dad ran his hand along the wall, his hard steps echoing. Reese said something to Phil and Phil took a big wad of cash from his back pocket and peeled off a few bills for him.

"Now what's this big room for?" my dad asked.

"This is my room," Reese said.

"Oh yeah? Where're the bunk beds?"

Reese gestured to the mop and bucket, the plastic carrier full of ninety-nine-cent cleaning supplies. "This is where I keep my supplies."

"Reese works for me," Phil said. "He's married to my niece."

Reese held up his hand beside his face like he was going to call to somebody across a gorge, but said nothing. He waggled a cheap golden wedding band.

"Well there you go," my dad said. "Nice to meet you, Reese."

Through the next door was a similar room full of flats of soda. Because the club was all-nude they couldn't serve alcohol.

"This just storage?" my dad asked.

"Uh-huh," Phil said.

"All right, let's see the dressing room."

The dressing room was tiny, about the size of three walk-in closets. It was crowded with a few thrift-store vanities and a set of lockers. An old tackle box full of glitter gloss and lipsticks sat out on the floor.

"*This* is your dressing room?"

Phil nodded.

Dad walked the narrow strip of concrete between all of the furniture. He stopped, bounced his butt back against the lockers. "How'm I supposed to get through here if I got ass, Phil?"

"I don't know."

"Egad," Dad said. He slapped off the lights. "Let's get out of here."

*　　*　　*

Back in the main room an older black guy was swelling out of his old suit, eyes pushing out of his face. He had a guitar case and was sipping from a soda can.

Phil walked to him, patted his back. "Good to see you, Ernie. How's it going?"

"Fine, fine." The words burbled up out of him. "You want me to start setting up?"

"Go for it."

When we walked past he reached out and grabbed my dad's shoulder. "I know you. I met you way back at Bourbon Street Circus."

"That's a good memory," my dad said. They shook hands.

"How've you been?" the guy asked.

"High and low and in between. How 'bout you?"

"Same as you. You going to stick around and watch me play?"

"Yes I am." Then Dad excused us and we went back to Phil's office.

My dad tapped his pipe out into Phil's ashtray. He put the pipe back inside his coat. "First off, that kid in there, the kid with the bucket."

"Reese."

"Fire him."

"Why?"

"Bad mojo, bad vibrations. There's something unnerving about him. I felt it and my son felt it." He gestured to me and I nodded. "Girl comes in here meets a kid like that she's not going to stick around. He's probably drilling holes in the wall, stealing bikini bottoms."

"He's married to my niece."

"Let that be her burden. I'm telling you that as long as you keep that kid around you're not going to be seeing the kind of girls that you want to see in here."

"You think that's it?"

"Part of it. Now, you know the room where he hangs out, with the mop and shit." Phil nodded. He was nodding this whole time, taking notes internal. "You need to hire somebody to remodel it and make a new dressing room. Find out if the wall between it and the storage is load-bearing and if it's not bust it down, make the place that much bigger. The nicer you make the dressing room the nicer the girls you'll get. If there's one thing I know about women, beautiful women, it's how much they appreciate a comfortable situation. You provide that for them, get rid of the creep, and the rest'll work itself out."

Phil blinked like a convert up from cold baptismal waters. "Well thank you, Will. You and your son are more than welcome to stick around for the entertainment if you want to. Couple of dances on the house, too." He pushed some carnival tickets toward us.

My dad didn't reach for them. "Why don't you save those for us until you get the pretty girls," he said.

Phil forced an embarrassed laugh. Dad stood.

"I'm just teasing, Phillip. We're going to come back and watch Ernie play, though. That we'll do."

We went to get hamburgers. "What about dinner?" I said. "They're going to get mad."

"That's okay. This guy we're going to see, you've never seen anybody play like him before."

I finished my burger, wadded up the wrapper. Sometimes I think weird things about burgers. About how many I've eaten, how many you'd have to stack up to make a cow. If it's worth it and how so.

We got back to the club just before Ernie went onstage. I took a chair flat against the wall and my dad sat across the room at a big round table with half a dozen college kids. There was a new girl on the smaller stage, all kinds of ugly. A few others were clip-clopping around on plastic stilettos and massaging dudes' shoulders, whispering sweet nothings and sour somethings. There were actually an unusual number of guys there that night—maybe twenty-five.

Then the loud rock faded down and the announcer, in his wannabe radio voice, introduced Ernie. When he came out and sat, a little bulb turned on above. He started strumming real slow, there in the pool of butter-colored light. The audience got half quiet, and the dancing girl stepped out of her underpants and started moving around as slow as the song, flashing it to the audience. Ernie's chords melted one into the other, and if you weren't listening close you wouldn't have heard the melody. The first song didn't make any sense, but it felt sad even though the lyrics were all desserts. "Fruit cake, cookie, sweet-potato pie," on and on like that. Like a menu.

At some point Ernie looked up from his guitar and met eyes with Phil standing a ways back. The last note was still reverberating through the speakers, filling the place like temperature, and he squeezed the neck of the guitar and choked it off. "I wrote a song for the owner of this place here," he said. The girl onstage gathered up her dollar bills, and swirling around on her hands and knees like that she looked sexy for maybe the first time in her life. "This song," he said, "is called 'Philly's Song.'"

He cleared his throat, took a long pull off of his Sprite that made me sure there was more than just soda in there. And then he starts into song number two. I'm pretty sure he was making it up right then and there if he hadn't just made it up in the bathroom.

"Lookit 'im there with his cute little hairdo, with his cute little face. Cheap son of a bitch named Philly Gelante. Cheap son of a bitch." It actually sounded kind of nice.

Phil stood there with his arms crossed, holding his elbows. Ernie played for another minute, until his subject turned his back to the stage and walked into the office. The second the door closed, Ernie said "That's Phillip Gelante, folks, give 'im a round of applause." A couple of jokers clapped, hooted. Ernie took more out of his soda can, thanked the boys for the applause, then started into another song, some old hat about a gambler. I guess you could say it was his fault for setting a playful tone. It did seem to sort of set a mood, to inspire what happened next.

First some dude up front flipped a book of matches at his feet. Ernie's eyes flashed down, but he ignored it. He played for another minute. Then the college boy straight across the table from my dad wads up a couple of wet cocktail napkins and sets them sailing toward the stage. The mess splats right into Ernie's knee, and he just stops playing. "Who did that," he says. It seemed funny at first. We all chuckled. "Who the fuck just threw that at my knee?" Ernie says. There was a mad-dog look in his eyes now.

I don't know why the college boy did what he did next. Maybe he was so milk-fed he'd never seen that look in a man's eyes before. Maybe they didn't have that look up in Alabaster Estates where he grew up. But for whatever reason or lack thereof, the big dumb kid raised his hand.

And with the urgency of a man who has to take a shit, Ernie dropped his guitar and threw his big fat body over the edge of the stage. He parted the crowd right to the college boy and sent him into the air hard and fast with one punch.

My dad turned to back away, but just sort of stumbled halfway up and plopped back into his seat. I jumped up and started toward him, but everyone was crowding around. The kid righted himself and Ernie hammered him so that he flopped back onto the table, drinks smash-splashing everywhere. The announcer was shouting for everybody to calm down. "Hey now, everybody chill! Be cool, guys, be cool!" still in that phony radio-DJ voice. I could see flashes of my dad through the crowd, sitting there, reaching out for something to steady himself on to stand. He was frightened. I wanted to throw him over my shoulder, carry him from harm's way, but I couldn't get there fast enough. There was an utter hopelessness in my stomach. Finally my dad grabbed one edge of the table and pushed himself to his feet. Ernie grabbed the opposite edge and flipped the whole thing with the kid on top. My dad slunched out of the way just in time. Half a second later and the table would've clipped him and split his head wide open. I pushed a guy in a bandanna aside and ran to him.

"Let's get out of here," he said, calmer than he should have been. Ernie picked up a stool and started hammering the kid's head into the ground. He hit him twice before the guy's friends grabbed onto his arms and started wrestling him down. On the way out I saw one of the strippers watching the fight and casually wiping her snotty nose with a wadded-up kleenex. I heard glass breaking and then we were out the door.

We walked over and leaned against the car. "Close one," I said.

"My legs don't work like they did when I was twenty-five." My dad was sixty-seven then and when he said that I saw him as an old man for the first time in my life.

He pulled the pipe from his pocket again, packed it, and held it to his bottom lip. Then he patted his pockets, turned to me. "Matches?"

I checked but didn't have any.

He slid the pipe back inside his coat. "Oh well."

A minute later Phil came running out. "I'm so sorry about that," he said, panting. "I'm really sorry."

My dad looked back toward the door, people shouting inside.

"Sounds like they want an encore."

Phil turned back to his club like he had no idea what could be going on in there. And looking at that strange and ugly place over this strange and ugly man's shoulder I was sure that the club would never succeed. The scene just screamed doom.

Phil turned and handed my dad an envelope. Pop flipped through the bills. "That's it?" He dropped the envelope on the pavement and flapped the money at Phil. "We didn't count on Ernie tearing the place up like that, did we? I'm an old man, I don't come out here to deal with this kind of shit, Phil. You get it? Lemme see that wad of yours."

"Well—"

"Come on, man."

Phil took the wad of cash from his back pocket, snapped the rubber band down around his wrist.

"That's right—peel some of that off for me, Phil. That was bullshit what happened in there. That table almost hit Will in the face."

On the way back to Tucson all the windows were up. It was totally black outside, red lights blinking on the mountaintops. Pop wasn't talking, just chewing, working through the bag of saltwater taffy

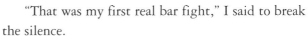

he'd picked up at the gas station.

"That was my first real bar fight," I said to break the silence.

"You missing a tooth?"

"What?"

"That wasn't a bar fight, Will. There wasn't even a real bar, for Christ's sake. That was just one man getting angry and a bunch of fools trying to watch." He shook his head. "Old Ernie. Jesus Christ."

"Was he always that hotheaded?"

"Well, yeah, but—you have to understand, they used to roll out the red carpet for that man. The girls used to line up." He sighed. The car rattled louder and I started imagining all the things going wrong inside of it that I was going to have to pay for. Then he reached over and pinched my neck. "Now you want to see a bar fight, get *me* mad." He smiled softly, raised his eyebrows. "Then you'll see a bar fight."

When we got back to the house the women stood there angry and without makeup. "Where were you?" said his new wife. Mine spoke scarier things with her eyes. She had the baby in her arms.

Seeing the women like that I stopped cold in my tracks, but my dad just showed his palms and kept his pace. His words were well delineated and calm, as if practiced a hundred times. "We went out, got drinks, we got drunk, we got dinner. I'm sorry, he's sorry." He pointed his thumb back at me and I nodded.

"You're a crazy old shit," his wife told him. She slapped his chest. I wouldn't get off as easy. But that was all it took for my dad to be absolved. That little bullshit speech, those strong old hands bared to her. They walked inside, not saying good-bye, and that was the last time I saw my old man standing.

MADNESS

by MATEI VISNIEC

THE TRANQUIL FOOL

OUR CITY WAS invaded by butterflies. They are huge, beautiful, carnivorous. We have never seen so many in the city. They have covered everything: streets, rooftops, cars, trees. People who were in the street during the invasion were eaten. From my window, I see three human skeletons and the skeleton of a dog, all picked perfectly clean. First the butterflies attack the eyelashes, the eyebrows, the eyelids, the lips, the vocal cords, and the taste buds. The most violently colored share all this. The others do the rest.

For the moment, the entire city is paralyzed. Our army could do nothing against the butterflies. We have had to get used to them. The people, entrenched in their homes, watch the butterfly-covered streets through their butterfly-covered windows. The little beasts seem to have definitively installed themselves in our city. They continue to flock here. The layer of butterflies becomes thicker and thicker. One could even call it colored snow.

Finally we figure out that the butterflies only devour those beings that make sudden movements. If we move very slowly, the butterflies don't react. We can even crush them underfoot; they remain calm and die silently. Incidentally, we can only get down the street by crushing them. Since they are extremely delicate, nearly transparent, the crushed butterflies gently dissolve to powder.

Life in the city continues in slow motion. It takes the General almost half an hour to cross the street. It takes the Colonel nearly two hours to reach the first bistro, just at the other end of the block.

As a result of this and our slowed thinking, we speak at a rate of one word a day. And when we make love, all goes quite slowly as well.

THE FEVERISH FOOL

The carnivorous butterflies were chased from the village by the pestilential snails. They came from everywhere: the bowels of the earth, canals, caves, sewers. They climb on walls and windows, leaving behind them a fine, viscous trail. They never eat anything, but the smell they give off is unbearable. In order not to collapse in the middle of the street from nausea, people run from place to place.

The problem with the pestilential snails is that they penetrate into our houses. We wake up in the morning, get out of bed, and our slippers are full of snails. We go to the bathroom and the sink is overflowing with snails. We cannot look at ourselves in the mirror because hundreds of snails have already collected there like gangrene. We go into the kitchen, cut the bread into slices, and inside the bread we find a pestilential snail. It is impossible to heat up a little milk or make a cup of coffee for oneself; in each pot there already lives an extremely mobile black snail with green horns. On each chair is a large pestilential snail, watching you with a guilty expression. They climb incredibly quickly on the furniture, on the curtains, and trail joyously across the ceiling. When we open a book, a tiny pestilential snail falls out. The old gramophone no longer works; the snails have made their nest there. Even drawers that have been locked with a key are crawling with snails with little hairs on their horns.

It was much better with the butterflies; everybody recognizes that now. We can no longer shake someone's hand, because a snail will always slide between the two palms, quick as lightning. When we buy the newspaper, it's almost certain that when searching for money in our pocket we will find a snail. The pestilential snails crushed underfoot and beneath car tires have formed a layer of soft sludge—blood and thin fibers of flesh.

Since people run all the time, they speak very little. Those who stop to exchange a few words, in spite of it all, risk immediate nausea. "The butterflies were so clean," says someone, spitting. "And they were so beautiful," replies another before vomiting.

To live with pestilential snails, you must first learn to be silent. Each word spoken leaves in its place, inside your mouth, a small pestilential snail.

THE LUCID FOOL

The pestilential snails were chased away by a gigantic and diffuse animal in the form of an odorless rain, falling incessantly on the city. People realized very quickly that this was no real rain, because there were no raindrops and no accumulation of water. The animal rain has saturated everything. It is now the living matter of the city: in the stone of the walls, in the glass of the windows, in the asphalt of the streets, in the wood of the trees, in the water of the canals, in the air that people breathe.

The animal rain takes nourishment from the substance of things. It empties, slowly and imperceptibly, everything that has a heart, a soul, meaning. The city is already full of dead bodies. It is useless to buy an apple; they are hollow inside. Bread is only crust, chickens lay transparent eggs. Trees are only inflated trunks. When we lift a rock, we find that it is strangely light. Fish float to the surface of the river, their skin containing only air. Every time a dog tries to bark, we hear only a sort of hissing, and sometimes we even see it collapse to the ground like a house of cards. The bronze of the statues has become as thin as a sheet of paper; the pedestals crumble under the weight of a bird.

The animal rain penetrates deeper and deeper, further and further. There is no shelter against it. People have tried everything: metal umbrellas, leather capes, underground bomb shelters, rebellion and silence. The animal rain now attacks time. No one can tell if it is day or night, if he is awake or asleep, if he is alone or being swallowed up in a crowd, if he is touching his own skin or the skin of another running alongside in the enormous conglomeration of empty beings.

The animal rain also lives in people's flesh, in their blood, in their gestures, and in their dreams. It is ubiquitous. It is inside each thought, each spoken word. You can hide nothing from it; it knows everything at every instant, day and night. It monitors all minds at the same time, because it breathes simultaneously in every mind. And it speaks with us, as if it were a second voice in our being. Its remarks are still rather primitive, like "You must not think of that, sir!" or "Oh, enough, you are going too far," or "It's dangerous to insist," or bluntly, "Let it go, that won't work either."

We deeply miss the time of the pestilential snails, which were at least very quiet.

Translated by Shari Gerstenberger

CUTS

by J. MALCOLM GARCIA

THE PHONE RINGS at the reception desk. Jay patches the call to me and I answer it.

"Out of the Rain, may I help you?" I say.

Nobody important. Just someone asking to donate clothes. Bring them down, I say. Park behind the building.

We don't need more used clothes. We have plenty. But if someone gives you clothes one day, they might give you a check the next. So you accept their clothes. After they drop them off, I'll ask a volunteer to take the clothes to Goodwill.

I hang up. It's 9 a.m. My program coordinator, Don, walks into the office and hands me a copy of a grant application he picked up at a downtown meeting of social-service providers. I hate meetings, so I send him.

I'm the director of Out of the Rain. We assist homeless mentally ill people. Shelter, referrals, counseling, job development—you name it. Twenty-four seven, we never close. We're also supposed to be the place that hires the homeless mentally ill so they can help their own.

Peer counseling, it's called. And every year, some of my counselors become clients because I lay them off. It goes both ways.

I throw the application on my desk. Don watches it slide almost right up to the edge. He calls himself the "codirector" because I include him in on my decisions, but he's not really my professional equal and he knows it.

"When's the deadline?" I ask him.

"Tomorrow noon."

"After today, we'll need it."

It's probably a job-development grant. Funding for agencies that help homeless people find work. We do that. Day labor, mostly. Very regular for my clients, very part-time. But it looks good on paper. I fudge the numbers to make the jobs sound like full-time gigs. Not misrepresenting anything, just suggesting conclusions not actually represented by the numbers. It's an art.

When I came into work this morning, I saw Billy, one of our clients, washing the windows of the fast-food joint across the street.

"How long you been working, Billy?" I asked him.

"Five minutes."

He climbed off the ladder and wiped his wet hands on his jeans. Soap bubbles popped on his beard. I offered him a smoke and he patted his pockets for matches.

"You going to be here all day?"

"Yeah."

"How much they paying you?"

"Food. I'm working for food, man. Can you believe it?"

"Oh well," I told him. "Beats a blank."

I made a mental note to include Billy in our monthly job stats. He said all day. Washing windows. That means eight hours as far as I'm concerned. That's a full-time maintenance gig in my book. Like I said, it's an art.

*　*　*

I lean back in my chair, look out the window. Billy's hard at it wiping down the aluminum awning now. I glance at my phone. The state assembly and governor agreed on a budget last night that will slash social services. The cuts will be passed on to cities. Our mayor will make noise about trying to absorb the cuts. How he'll lobby the governor. Sometimes he means it. Sometimes it helps but not much. A few thousand dollars saved here and there. Not enough. Never has been. Once all the posturing is out of the way, we'll get a call. Nonprofit agencies like mine with state contracts will feel the knife.

It always boils down to cutting staff, something my contract forbids. It doesn't look good for a helping agency to terminate employees. So we don't. Instead, my personnel manual allows for "transition opportunities."

In the past, I've made these opportunities available to staff who had a chance of getting work elsewhere. Staff with some education, skills, work history. But after years of transition opportunities, I'm pretty much out of people like that.

I don't have any more Poppa Rons. Poppa Ron told me he'd been a trucker before he lost his job and landed on the streets. A big old dude in a cowboy hat, jeans, and a T-shirt. He had a Santa Claus beard and a wallet full of pictures of his eight kids, all with different mothers, he told me, all scattered across the country. Poppa Ron I suspect lost his truck-driving job from drinking, because every afternoon he got off work he tied one on to the point I'd find him passed out on the street and have to help him to his room in a beat-down residential hotel around the corner from our office. But he always made it to work five minutes before his shift started. Kept the referrals flowing and prevented fights before they happened.

Without him, now, the front desk gets backed up. We run out of referral slips, and my remaining staff take it personally when someone gets in their face. Then I find myself running down the stairs screaming, "Let it go, let it go!" before someone throws a punch.

Desperate people come into this place and all I have left is jittery help. Most don't show up on time for their shifts because they started using again, because they were busted for drugs, because the voices inside their head said Fuck it. Ron had enough of a grip on himself to work an eight-hour day before he indulged his self-destructive impulses.

Our clients are crazy, not stupid. They understand the message, when someone gets let go: we're all expendable.

There is Don, though. He could easily get another job. College educated, master's degree in theology and sociology. Never been homeless. He's lived as middle-class an existence as I have. That's what drew us together. Initially anyway. Us against the crazies.

When I let Ron go he told me he couldn't drive anymore. He didn't have a license. It's always something.

I consider my staff list and put a question mark by Don's name.

The reception desk phone rings. Jay transfers the call to me.

"Out of the Rain, may I help you?"

It's my girlfriend, Jean. I tell her I'll call her back. It's almost noon now.

"She hates this time of year with the budget," I tell Don. "Knows I'll be working late."

"Go home," he says. "I'll let you know if they call."

"No. Thanks."

Two years ago, I drove home before the call came. My head

wouldn't rest. How bad would it be? When would I know? Eventually I gave up on sleeping and went back to Out of the Rain to spend the night in the shelter. Don was there. We fretted into the wee hours, sleepless, brought together through a shared fear that neither Jean nor anyone else understood. We smoked cigarettes and drank coffee and asked the same questions over and over again. How bad? How bad?

When we began to fade and fall asleep despite ourselves, I walked out with Don to my car. I drove home and found Jean buried beneath the pillows. Light from the street seeped through the blinds. Her mouth was barely open. I bent to kiss her neck, but she dug deeper under the sheets and raised a limp hand and pushed my face to one side. I slid into bed but couldn't sleep. I got back up and went into the kitchen and made a sandwich. I swatted at flies bouncing off the light above the sink. I stared at the dark outline of my reflection in the living room window. I couldn't see my face. A vast darkness populated by lights stretched into infinity. I dozed, my sandwich half-eaten on my lap, and awoke later to a fog-diluted sunrise. Birds chirped in emotionless repetition. A blue haze of humidity hung everywhere. I opened the back door to a windless day. Just a heaviness in the air waiting to break. I wondered if Don had slept. I wrapped what remained of my sandwich in cellophane and went to bed.

When I woke up again, Jean was already at work. A towel thrown over the bedpost, a cup of coffee in the sink, the newspaper on the kitchen table revealed her morning to me but little else.

Don watches me examine the staff list.

"Did I see you mark my name?"

"I'm just counting."

I won't lie and say no. But there's no point saying yes either. I am counting. How do we stay open twenty-four hours with further staff cuts? How many can go before that's impossible? So yes, I'm counting. I tap my pen by each name. Do I need them? What happens to them if I don't?

Don is a recovering alcoholic. HIV positive. Last month he applied for a counseling supervisor position at the AIDS Foundation. He's one of three finalists for the job. He likes to imagine what his life will be like if he gets it. Telling people what to do. *I'm the supervisor now*, he'll say, rehearsing a hypothetical conversation with a contrary staff member. *I'm in charge*. The foundation director told him he would decide by the end of today. I hope they offer it to him. It would allow me to cut a staff position without causing any pain.

Don doesn't appear sick. He's thin. As thin as he was three years ago during his interview. He came in late his first day at work, said he had a flat. He was unshaven. I wondered if he'd had a slip. But he didn't smell of booze and he was never late again. That night, on his way home, a mugger jumped him, held a knife to his back and demanded his wallet. One of Don's new business cards fell out and the mugger picked it up. When he saw Don worked at Out of the Rain, he apologized and returned the wallet. He had crashed in our shelter several times, he said. He asked for a referral but Don refused. Then he walked away, pausing to apologize again one last time. Even a mugger understood the importance of this place.

The reception desk phone rings. Two thirty.

"For you," Jay shouts, and transfers the call.

A Salvation Army counselor asks me if we have spare bus tokens. I tell her I'm tapped out. Don and I agreed to give out just five a day. Otherwise we'd run out too fast.

Ginger, our benefits advocate, pokes her head into my office.

"Nothing," I say when I hang up. "It wasn't them."

Ginger sighs and asks for the copy key to print her stats.

My staff doesn't often use the copy machine; I don't let them. Clients who need to makes copies of their birth certificates, social security cards, IDs, whatever, for some benefit application—they have to go elsewhere so we can save money on paper.

"What do you think?" Ginger asks.

"That I won't know until I know."

Ginger was homeless two years ago, diagnosed with schizophrenia. We helped her get disability. She saw a doctor, got on meds, stopped hearing voices, and enrolled in a job-training program that allowed her to remain eligible for disability for one year from her hire date if the job didn't work out. I hired her a year ago tomorrow, about the same time I took on Jay. I fired Shelly to do it.

Shelly was our in-house alcoholism counselor when we had staff members falling off the wagon by the trainload. But by the time she started we had plateaued into semi-stability. Staff either got in recovery and stayed there or spiraled off into the street, never to return. Shelly had little to do, and showed no initiative in doing any of it, other than chatting with friends on the phone. So when our budget was cut last year, I used that as an excuse to give her the boot. She was tearful. I told her it had nothing to do with her job performance. It did, of course, and she knew it, but I had enough heart not to rub it in. She was a nice gal.

I wish I had a few more easy ones, a few more Shellys. I heard she got married and has a kid on the way. She's doing all right.

*   *   *

The reception desk phone rings. Jay sends it through. Three o'clock.

"Out of the Rain, may I help you?"

An Episcopal Sanctuary volunteer asks me if I have bus tokens. One of his clients needs a ride to Walgreens to fill a prescription.

"Sorry," I say, "I don't."

Ginger looks through the door.

"It wasn't them," I tell her.

She purses her lips, turns away from me. I hear her mutter something to herself and then cover her mouth. She looks at the floor. Her cheeks twitch and she hurries back to her office. Last year she organized a staff Christmas party at her apartment. I'll never forget that bathroom—the raw, acidic funk. Kitty litter and cat shit filled the tub. It hadn't been cleaned in God knows how long. I pulled the shower curtain closed. Even when Ginger had it together, cracks showed. I never did see a cat.

"Sad," Don says, watching Ginger. "So sad."

For a while Jean and I and Don and his partner Jerry socialized. We got together at Thanksgiving and Christmas. More often, Don and I took our lunch breaks together and saw movies after work. We watched each other's apartments when one of us went on vacation. I'd feed his cat on the way back from work and sit on his living room couch and listen to it eat until it had finished. I read postcards Don sent from Hawaii, Florida, wherever he and Jerry ended up. When I finished, I stuffed them in my pocket and continued sitting.

In the expanding silence that followed, I'd imagine what it was like to be Don. Getting up in the morning and slipping into the designer jeans he liked to wear. Tucking in his shirt and tying his shoes. Grabbing his briefcase. Going out the door. What did he think at those moments? Did he kiss Jerry good-bye?

Last December, before Ginger's party, Don and I spent a weekend afternoon at his house, writing Christmas cards to our staff. We didn't have money for a holiday bonus, so I decided personal handwritten notes from one of us would at least show we appreciated them. Don and I sat on the floor with cards and envelopes strewn at our feet, sunlight cutting through the blinds.

"I'll write the notes to the paid staff, you take the volunteers," I said.

"Aren't we both writing notes to everyone?"

"That would take forever. You take volunteers and I'll take staff."

"Why don't we split them? Half volunteers, half staff. Each of us."

"No."

"Why? I supervise them."

"Yeah? Who fires them?"

Don didn't answer.

"The paid staff need to hear from me because I'm the one who told them there would be no bonus this year. You get the volunteers. They weren't expecting anything. Not even a card."

I picked out one showing Santa Claus scrambling down a chimney, a huge stuffed sack thrown over one shoulder. Smiling reindeer stood with him on the snowbound rooftop. Don stood up and went into the kitchen. He opened a cabinet and took out a glass and filled it with Pepsi. He drank by the kitchen sink without offering me anything. I opened the card and wrote *Dear Don*. It was all so petty, really, when I think about it.

I came to Out of the Rain after directing a Salvation Army homeless shelter. My first day there, my supervisor asked me how long I'd been sober. Most of the staff had been hired from halfway houses for newly recovering alcoholics. It was just an assumption that everyone working in the shelter had been a homeless alcoholic. Like saying good morning. *How long you been sober?*

I said two years, afraid to reveal who I really was: a child of the suburbs, a church volunteer and a Cub Scout. My mother made me snacks after school, then rushed around the house to finish chores in time for dinner.

"Lord, I have a thousand and one things to do!" she would declare when the phone rang. Then she would dash through the kitchen and out the back door to the yard, scattering the air above her head with her hands and instructing me to say that she was out. She'd stand out there and press her face against the pane in the door, lipping with exaggerated puckerings and stretchings of her mouth—Who is it?—as I explained that my mother was out and no, she shouldn't be out too long.

Years later, I attended college on my parents' dime and received a degree in social work because a friend told me most of my time would be filled with internships instead of lectures.

My "recovery" became part of my professional persona. The story circulated and was expanded with details I had never offered. It gave me street cred. I never corrected it.

When I started working at Out of the Rain, though, I fell into the habit of stopping by the Comeback Club for a beer on my way home. The Comeback was blocks from my office and dark inside. Anyone glancing through the windows wouldn't see me. Some nights, when Jean would ask me to come straight home and take her to dinner, I'd agree but stop at the Comeback anyway for a quick one, maybe a couple of shots of Jack Daniel's. Down a small can of V8 juice on my way home to kill my breath.

Don saw me at the Comeback Club one afternoon. The door was open to the sidewalk and he walked inside through a stream of sunlight. He gave the bartender two dollars and got change. Maybe he needed it for the bus. I was at a table, waiting to order a beer and a sandwich. Don did a double-take when he saw me. I didn't look at him. I watched Don without looking at him directly. He left without a word.

He could threaten my job if he said anything to my executive director. He holds that over me.

I want to know why Don was at the Comeback Club. He could get change anywhere. Maybe he'd been chipping all this time and I never knew. Maybe he was planning to buy a drink before he saw me. He thought quickly, changed course, got change. Smooth. With his diagnosis, he has good reason to drink. I'm just saying. Makes me think.

The reception phone rings. 4 p.m.

"The shelter needs you to order more blankets," Jay shouts, and hangs up.

"Okay," I say, and make a note for myself. Then I ball it up and throw it in the trashcan. I don't have money for blankets.

Don and I stopped getting together after work when the state began its budget slashing. It was too awkward. How could I have dinner with him one night when I might cut him the next? The job came first. We understood that then and still do.

He hasn't told anyone about his diagnosis other than Jerry and me. On the day his doctors confirmed it, he came into my office and wept. I felt badly for him, but I also thought of my budget.

"If there's anything I can do," I told him.

Don was hospitalized for three days with a fever a while back.

Collapsed at home. Jerry called me. I drove to the hospital. Friends crowded Don's room. They filed up to his bed one at a time and embraced him.

"Don," I said, when it was my turn. I put my hand on his knee. "Get better. Now."

 He gripped my hand, eyes closed. The strength still in his arm surprised me.

"Tom," he said to me. "Don't worry. I love you. I didn't see anything."

I don't know—I didn't expect it. I responded without thinking—I whispered, "I love you, too." And then I did think about it. I let go of his hand and stepped back. Another one of his friends embraced him. I excused myself and hurried out.

"Will you miss me if I get the job?" Don asks me now.

I look out the window. Billy's hosing down the sidewalk. I have been missing Don for some time, but I don't care to speak about it.

"Let's wait and see if they call," I say.

The reception desk phone rings. Jay sends it through. Almost 5 p.m. now.

"Shelter referral," I tell Don and hang up the phone.

Ginger walks down the hall, talking loudly to Jay, and then bursts into high-pitched laughter. Jay cringes. Ginger unties her ponytail and pulls her hair behind her head. She jerks it several times, sending jolts through her face. Then she ties it off and stares at Jay as if he were a complete stranger. He covers his face.

"Jay, you okay?" I ask him.

"Yes," he says into his hands. "Get her away from me."

"Ginger, write up a shelter referral for a guy from Goodwill who's coming over."

She stares at me hard and lets out a long breath as if it's all she can do not to scream at me. Starts undoing her ponytail again.

The phone rings. Jay answers.

"Jean," he shouts.

"Tell her I'll call her back, Ginger, the referral. Now, please."

"The front desk needs sign-in sheets," Jay shouts to me.

I should call Jean. Last year she accepted a job with a corporate law firm. Suddenly she was working nine to five, not nine to nine. Suddenly her colleagues were not welfare-rights advocates but men and women with families. Suddenly she wanted all of that with me. A house, not a rental. Children instead of clients. A social life instead of twelve-hour days.

At this point, Jean doesn't think much of Out of the Rain.

What good do you do? she asks me. What enjoyment do you get out of it? What are you doing there that someone else couldn't do?

She was a law student when we met, at a social-services commission meeting. Her black curly hair unfurled to her shoulders and behind her self-effacing attitude she had a mind that could rattle off flaws in the system as easily as I could hum a tune. We flirted until I found the gumption to ask her out one February afternoon. All the restaurants were full. We bought a box of greasy take-out chicken, sat in her apartment, and talked deep into the night. When we got drunk enough, we took a bubble bath together. A year and a half later, we rented a house.

I can't just walk away, I tell her.

She has a point, though. We don't provide much besides a drop-in center now. We're more of a holding pen than a program.

I could cut myself and leave the whole mess to Don. I doubt he'd take it given his diagnosis, but maybe. Stress isn't something he needs, but if the AIDS Foundation job falls through, what would he have to lose? He could assume my position and keep looking for work elsewhere, and I would be an example of compassionate leadership remembered by them all. I cut myself to save some of you.

But what would I do? Would I find another job where I could hire the Jays and Gingers of the world? Would Don hire them? And if he wouldn't, where would they go, what would they do? I can't hire anyone now, but I can try to hang on to those I still have.

The reception desk phone rings. Jay points a finger at me like a conductor singling out a violin player. 6 p.m.

"Out of the Rain, may I help you?"

Another request for a bus token. Somebody trying to get to a detox outside the city. They'll sell the token and buy a drink, I'm sure. But I'm tired of saying no. I shout for Ginger and tell her to leave a token at the front desk.

"Why're you doing that?" Don asks.

"Giving a guy a break."

"We agreed not to give out more than five tokens a day. That's six."

"All right, so what? Jesus, Don, what does it matter?"

"Because if I tell the staff no more tokens, what good is it if you override me? You and Jerry. You're both the same. Do I not have a say in anything?"

I don't answer.

"Do I?" he says again.

"It's a fucking bus token, Don. It's—"

The reception desk phone rings. Don walks away. Jay answers and then puts down the receiver.

"Wrong number," he says.

Ginger comes to the door. Her eyes loom hugely behind her glasses. She has put on lipstick, smearing it beyond her mouth.

"Everyone's listening to you and Don," she says, handing me the referral. "Look outside. See them staring up at you? Nothing you decide will be a secret. It's in the stars. Carried by electrical currents. We already know."

Her voice trails off and she leaves, head thrust back, chest pushed out, arms outstretched as if she expected hands to reach down through the ceiling and lift her up and out of here. I go over my staff list and put a question mark by her name. Then I cross it out. She may never come down from whatever planet she's on, no matter what happens. Disability needs to know her status. She needs to know. I have to make choices. I draw a line through her name.

I glance outside, don't see Billy. A CLOSED sign hangs in the restaurant window. Homeless men line the sidewalk to sign up for our shelter, unaware I may have to cut our hours.

I start reading the grant application. Might as well fill it out. I'm not going home. No point. I open a desk drawer for my job stats folder. Need to add Billy's name. I should call Jean.

Don rolls his cell phone in his hand. I hear him tap, tap, tap it against the desk.

"Well," he says, speaking as if he's in the middle of a thought, "I'll miss you."

He gets up and tells Jay to take a break. He sits at the reception desk. He looks at me and then turns away. He starts dialing. Who's he calling? There is a possibility, I know, that he has already spoken to my executive director. That it's already in motion. It would be so easy if it happened like that. I'd be out of here for a reason my staff would appreciate. Tom had a slip. I didn't abandon them, I was fired. They'd understand. But it's his word against mine. Sure, I was at the Comeback Club. Doesn't mean I was drinking. I had ordered a sandwich. All true. And why, I would ask my executive director, did Don choose a bar of all places to get change?

I'm covered. I've got my story.

I go over my staff list again and stop at Don's name. *T.O.*, I write.

I imagine Don sitting at home in clothes getting too large for him. Month after month. Losing weight. Taking his meds. Jerry by his side. Shrinking while I'm here alone with no budget, no staff. Only homeless volunteers left to run the joint. But I will be keeping the doors open. I will be doing that much.

Jay starts chuckling to himself. He pauses to look at me and laughs louder. I don't even question what he's thinking.

The reception phone rings. Don looks at it. He rests his hand on the receiver but does not answer. Ginger and Jay and I watch him.

 Ginger grasps Jay's hand. Waiting. Don ignores the phone and us.

After a moment, I write Billy's name into the stats. Eight hours, full time. I listen to the phone ring again, echoing down the hall. Don's right. Let it ring. Ring all goddamn night if need be. It's all the same no matter what they tell me. I just go with the numbers.

FOOTHILL BOULEVARD

by CATHERINE BUSSINGER

THE THING WAS to get the list and go for a little ride. Fixate on one. One or two. Three, tops. Mad Dog explained it to me in unnecessary detail. He ticked off points in the phlegmy, gravel-choked voice I hated, like George C. Scott in *Patton*, slapping at the list with one hand as he lay sprawled back on the twisted bedding. The sheets were gray and limp, creased with grime, translucent from too many washings with cheap suds, and this nearly satisfied my need for contempt in this situation.

Ten minutes earlier Mad Dog had paused for effect like a gymnast, poised over me, balancing his weight on his elbows. His biceps had tensed and bulged against my temples, round and hard as Gravensteins, exploding with upraised veins like wriggly blue snakes. Look at that, he had said, jutting his chin at the stereo display, reveling in his own vitality. Man, would you just look at that, he said, and I felt the sneer distorting the panel of my upper lip.

What, you don't like that?

The constant preening and posing was vulgar to me. Unseemly.

I couldn't use it right then. His vanity was childish. It wasn't manly. And that was acceptable because he wasn't a serious contender for my heart, which in any event had been wrapped, stamped, and parcel-posted to parts unknown. I was a lost soul.

Well, you don't have to *eat* it, he'd said. In no way had my donkeyish balking dimmed his enjoyment of the miracle of himself—alive at that moment, inside of me; like a usurping army.

Now I was already up and dressed. I snatched the list from his hand and smoothed it out on the table. This was in what had been Mad Dog's Top Choice from last year's list; we're talking about houses here. Property auctioned off by the county for unpaid taxes.

The plan was simple: you get the list, you go for a drive; you go to the courthouse, you bid on your house. For a few thousand dollars—the paltry sum the pitiful Owner of Record hadn't been able to scrape together—the house was yours. This was a while back, of course. Before real estate in the Bay Area went into orbit.

The houses were always in the shittiest neighborhoods. The ones you could get, I mean. Junkies stumbling around like the Dawn of the Dead. Homeless people squatting on curbs, none of them enterprising enough to even own a shopping cart. On every corner loose gangs of young males stood rotating like seagulls, staring with hard eyes, squawking, ready to fly at you. There were a couple of addresses in decent areas, but those would invariably be redeemed. One three-story Spanish-style in North Berkeley had somehow ended up on the list; that was the one I could see myself in, up in the arched window of that faux bell tower. Mad Dog said forget about it. Don't even waste your time. On the day of the auction, the docket number was called out from the list of those reclaimed by owners, and one hundred people got up and walked out without a word. That house stands a couple blocks down the road from the white wedding-cake Victorian where I, having kicked and clawed my way up the hill in the intervening years, now live.

Some of the addresses on the list, you don't even slow down. Just shacks. Or charred piles of toppled bricks where people used to hang up Christmas stockings and sit down every night for dinner together. At one property, a scrawny old man in a droopy, sleeveless undershirt brushed back the rust-stained curtain as I coasted to a stop. He peered out at me with saggy, crusted eyes and slack lips and I popped the clutch and peeled out just as Mad Dog raised his styrofoam cup of coffee to take a sip. "You sure take off in a hurry," he said, dabbing at his steaming shirt.

You could take away someone's home. This is what Mad Dog had done the previous year. Morris Peacock, cantankerous South Berkeley stumblebum, had owned the cockeyed kelly-green Queen Anne on the corner of Fairview and Whatnot for half of the last century. Now it belonged to Mad Dog. He had a permanent bald spot on the back of his head as a souvenir from the exchange: Morris had hunted him down the day after the auction and beaned him with a clinker brick he'd pried from the chimney. This contretemps was a source of genuinely injured feelings for Mad Dog.

The house I ended up with was a grab bag. An abandoned, plywood-clad brown shingle on Foothill Boulevard in Oakland, where the annual murder rate is in the triple digits. At the courthouse, when the docket number was called, no one bid against me. This might have concerned me but for the fact that an hour before the auction, Mad Dog and I had descended on the house with crowbars, prying away a corner of the sheathing. I wiggled through the slot while Mad Dog levered the bar. In the jolting yellow dot of my flashlight I saw what I saw. I had some money saved from waitressing nights at a Turkish restaurant on Telegraph Avenue, money that was earmarked for when I got into graduate school. At the courthouse I raised my hand and bid three thousand dollars, the amount of taxes due, plus one dollar, and then I was a woman of property.

Back on Foothill we ran through the dark empty house whooping and shrieking. Rosewood paneling, hardwood floors, a long, sloping sunporch. I lifted my heel and kicked out the plywood panel covering the kitchen windows; light poured in, greedily fingering surfaces that had been denied it for too long. That every pane of glass, including what would turn out to be three hundred 6" × 8" panes on the sunporch, had been painstakingly broken, that every possible removable fixture—cabinets, doors, sinks, tub, toilet, water heater—had been systematically stripped away and carted off by someone with ample time and power meant little to me; this was a thing I could fix. I could do this. And then I would have something.

I needed that. I needed to prove that I could do something, that I could take a thing that someone else had discarded and rescue it.

 The air inside was clogged with flying dust. Mad Dog went out, coughing and cawing, crowbar in hand; I followed after, cupping my hand to my face. There were squad cars surrounding the porch. A half dozen cops, some crouching behind their doors, had their guns pointed at me. I was squinting in the sunshine and must have had what looked like a big, stupid, drugged-out smile on my face.

The officer at the foot of the stairs was yelling something. He had a wet, red face and was spitting mad, but I could see that under the ruby flush his skin was the pale, lifeless gray of plastic computer components, and I was thinking that someone should probably tell him to go in for a monitored stress test before he keeled over. I turned my head and saw Mad Dog spread-eagled against the front wall of the house, his chin down like he was crying into his shoulder, his monster deltoids straining at the insufficient little caps of white sleeve.

"Step over and put your hands on the wall with your partner!" the cop yelled, his face contorting with the effort of forming syllables at top volume.

"Wait," I said. "Wait a second. I just bought this house."

The cop whipped around to look toward a man standing on the sidewalk, who shook his head in disgust, negating this notion. If the man had been a little closer I could have read the name scribbled in yellow like egg drool across the pocket of his mechanic's overalls—BERT. He had his arms folded way up high and tight over his belly, and a lock of wavy white hair dipping over his forehead like a rooster comb. All I could think of was Foghorn Leghorn.

"Here," I said, "I've got the papers in my pocket," and foolishly moved to retrieve them. There was a mad flurry of clicking safeties. Mad Dog made a high pitched canine sound in his throat.

I can see now that this is the type of thing you read about in the newspaper, the type of thing that happens fairly regularly in that part of town—someone behaving foolishly, thoroughly misjudging and mistaking the situation and ending up dead. I got lucky that day, although I didn't realize it at the time; I was incredulous, and vaguely insulted. I was moving way too fast; I had a lot to do, and these cops were in my way, and they were going to feel pretty stupid in a minute, I believed. Looking back I can only shake my head. I didn't have the slightest inkling of my new rank.

Officer Cardiac Arrest edged up and, with two fingers, almost delicately, yanked the paper from my hand. Went into a semi-crouch in order to read.

Okay, he said, finally. Okay. He stood and put his gun back in his holster, and the others followed suit. A few of the officers looked disappointed; their shoulders slumped. The red-faced cop  reached to hand back my receipt, then stepped off the porch, squinting up at me for a long minute, his mouth working as though he was about to say something, and I thought he might apologize. Instead, he turned away, and soon they were all chatting amicably with each other or babysitting their spitting two-ways, burping them against their shoulders. Then they got in their squad cars and drove off.

The man with the name tag remained standing on the sidewalk, rocking back on his heels. This was my introduction to the neighborhood blowhard who owned the tire shop next door and upon whose whims and courtesies and sense of punctilio I would be dependent for the next several epochs. "You have no idea," he said. "You've got absolutely no idea what you've done."

When I turned I saw Mad Dog, still starfished against the house.

I remember the first time I saw my house. I was peering through the windshield, driving up Foothill Boulevard searching for the address printed on the assessor's list. It stood out, with its bay window and sloping roof, and I felt a stirring when I saw it. I don't remember much about the drive or the approximately one hundred other properties I glanced at and rejected that day. The event was overlaid with the intense melancholy of having to spend a prolonged period of time in a confined space with Mad Dog, who seemed to me to be continually striking a pose with his very white cigarettes and his very black coffee and his very white teeth and his miraculous sheaf of platinum hair and his pinwheel eyes that were green and green and green. Which normally, I like. It's my favorite; it's my type. Which was why I had thought, erroneously as it turned out, that Mad Dog with his movie-star good looks might be able to woo my heart away from the clutches of my True Love, a man as far outside the parameters of my physical ideal as it was possible to be, which inconsonance had merely fueled my conviction, clearly *proved* to me that what I felt for him was genuine and inescapable and predetermined and correct and wholly outside of my control. My True Love was a man twelve years my senior who had romanced me mercilessly for six months, right up until the moment he told me we could no longer see each other for reasons that were confusing to me. As I say, my heart was a twisted, crumpled-up thing. It was causing me genuine physical pain. I had heard of an incident on the freeway where a lug wrench sailed off the bed of a tow truck and came crashing through some guy's windshield, slugging him in the chest, and I believed that I knew how he'd felt. The man had survived, but just barely.

Mad Dog strode around unshaven in strategically torn Levi's and big shit-stomping motorcycle boots. He had an ebony-inlaid derringer he liked to make a show of cleaning at his kitchen table, quoting from the Old Testament in a Kentucky-fried Kingfish voice: Bring me a chalice of solid gold! Bring me an altar of solid *gold!* Waving the gun around, drawing a bead on the light fixture.

But Mad Dog was just camping out here. Slumming it. He was aplayin' the desperado. It came as sorry, late news to me that I'd invested the remaining coin of my romantic fortune in a counterfeit. Under the dangerous veneer he was a mama's boy, a person of privilege, a Mr. Fussyfussywuss—the spoiled scion of some hotshot, moneyed Washington, DC politico, educated to the teeth at MIT. A poseur with a prim and persnickety sense of entitlement. That was Mad Dog; and for that reason I dub him, ironically, Mad Dog.

And who was I? A small-town girl, misplaced. Dirty-blonde, dull and hateful; sorely miseducated and pissed-off about it—Art, Art History, *French*; in what real-world scenario had I believed these subjects could buoy me? I needed to be smart here. I needed to be looking out for an angle. I still had a smattering of what seemed to me to be a quickly diminishing store of charm. I could spread it thin; I could fit the role, for a short while, of the blonde shiksa sexpot opposite Mad Dog's bad-boy act. We looked good together; we both went along with that as far as it would go.

This seems to be the story of my life: a refusal to enjoy the flavor of what was on my plate in anticipation of the feast that never came.

The house was in what Mad Dog called *an area of increased pigmentation*. I was a novelty, with my melanin-deficient pallor and stringy hair that was neither styled or processed, my clothes that were soon filthy beyond belief, day after day crusted with roofing tar and spackling paste and stuff that looked like bird droppings. "Girl, don't you got you no other clothes?" a thin young woman who paced the sidewalk in red tube top and pedal pushers asked me confidentially one day, keeping her eyes carefully blank to show that, if I didn't, well, that was all right.

Gangs of children roamed the neighborhood; they slowed as they passed the house, staring and hooting. They moved in flocks, dif-ferentiated by size and plumage the way several different breeds of birds can occupy a territory without intermingling. Latchkey kids, truants, illegal immigrants. They gravitated to the house quite naturally, drawn by the assortment of violent, noisy, dangerous power tools, the wholesale destruction inside. Hey lady, Alfredo said. Hey lady, what we doin today? He had some English; his many small siblings had none. They squabbled fiercely like magpies over the hammer, clasping it tight like a baby doll.

I was living on fun-size Snickers and Midol, which I found to give a powerful physical and psychological boost essential to the twelve to fourteen hours a day I was to spend mindlessly sawing and hammering, digging, grinding, swabbing, scrubbing, plastering, sanding, painting, and sobbing disconsolately into my filthy, ruined hands. At dusk I boarded the place back up and piled all my tools into my car and drove home to my rented apartment where my roommates were sitting around at the kitchen table in clean clothes with freshly washed hair waiting for dinner. They had drawn up a cleaning/cooking/groceries schedule and I really needed to make a better effort to comply. Megan in particular was royally pissed in a new, junior-managerial way. Was I even aware that tonight was my night to cook?

Meanwhile it was the grimy sheets again. Mad Dog cupped my head in his hands, surreptitiously flexing his biceps. In the golden light his eyes were topaz shot with emerald, the irises iridescent, constantly changing, like semiprecious stones, like tigereye agate. Why is this night different from all other nights? he intoned, giving me his satanic smile. He said this every time. At first, the Passover reference had been lost on me. I didn't know he was mocking his Jewish heritage; I thought he meant something. Sometimes I felt that maybe this would work, that maybe everything would be all right, if I could just somehow get him never to speak ever again.

Earlier that day Mad Dog had come by to see my house freshly unsheathed. Had struck a pose at the top of the drive, hands

wedged in his pockets. Had whistled through his teeth while looking queasy. Man, that's a project and a half, he'd said, and, That
roof's gonna go anytime, and Why'd you put the shut-off valve *after*
the water heater?

At some point, staring up at the looming face of the house,
Mad Dog's eyes clouded over. Whatever you do, he said, don't ever
let any building inspectors into the place. They'd rip it to shreds.

And then he had to go. He had troubles of his own.

I had other visitors. Lee and Lonnie lived in the yellow stucco next
door. Twins, eleven years old, big for their age. They specialized in
apparating silently in doorways, arm in arm like Tweedledee and
Tweedledum. Handsome kids with excellent posture, clean, pressed,
color-coordinated clothes, and something wrong with them, some
deficit that expressed itself in twin staring without expression. They
conversed only with each other, speaking of me in the third person,
snorting with muffled, secret bursts of laughter.

Hush, fool! She's lookin' at you!

Act cool, she's Wonder Woman, Lee hissed once, as a section of
waterlogged wallboard peeled away in my hands.

 They had a skinny sidekick who scared me. Curtis had
a wizened, wrinkled face and angry, asymmetrical eyes.
A head shorter than Lee and Lonnie but he was the front
man—antic, manic, sizzling with barely suppressed rage.
Lee and Lon attendant upon his scorn, upon his slapping,
kicking fury.

"Okay," he said, nodding grimly a couple dozen times, the first
time they brought him. "This is my crib. This where I put my TV,
dig? Stereo, boom box," he said, shimmying, waving his hand to the
corners. Glaring murderously at me.

Lee and Lonnie were impressed. Had no plan of their own. Or any plan to have a plan.

When I set the heavy paper-wrapped package of new windowpanes delicately on the steps and turned to pick up my caulking gun, the porch tilted, rotted through at the base, and fifty 6" × 8" panes of glass smashed to pieces on the pavement. On cue, Bert rolled around the corner of his garage like he was on wheels, making a show of swallowing a smirk. The tongue of white hair bobbed, teasing his yellow beak of a nose, and I focused on that: it was a ridiculous foofoo feather on a hat, he was a ridiculous bozo-man, and he wasn't going to see me cry. Bert pointedly ignored the broken glass, locked his knees, and gazed toward the intersection, beyond the place two doors up where a car had come hurtling off Foothill Boulevard spinning like a bottle, taking out a chunk of the building like a bite from a piece of birthday cake; that was old news, that was not of interest. Now he spoke with covert delectation, unmistakable *nyah-nyah*, of a robbery that had taken place the night before at the gas station visible if I was only to rise up slightly on the balls of my feet. Told how the new young owner and his idiot wife had already closed for the night when someone rapped on the bulletproof glass asking for change for a twenty. How the stupid little woman had reached to unlock the door as the husband shouted No! No!, too late to stop her, and the robber pulled a gun and blasted the man's brains out while the silly woman screamed and screamed.

A young guy was locomotoring past on the sidewalk, on his way to somewhere else.

"And it didn't have anything to do with you being *black* and *me* being *white*, son!" Bert yodeled, incorporating this random passerby into his soliloquy. Bert had a custom-made message for everyone: his specious, self-serving message for the young guy was *We're all in this together*; his message for me was *You're all alone out here.* The young man kept his eyes straight, kept moving, made a stiff, careful semi-circle around Bert, skirting the crazy man.

"Yip. Yip, yip, yip, yip, yip. Yessiree Bob. You're a real liability to me here," Bert said, squinting down at me as if from a dizzying height, snarling his nose at me like a terrier. "You're a bad-news bear. You're gonna get me killed. Two more years till I retire, and now *this*." A dramatic sweeping gesture of disgust toward me, the house.

I could mark the passing hours of each day by which kids were camped out in my new house. Alfredo brought his little posse by in the early afternoon, stood in the center of the dining room with his hands on his hips, his face lit with mischief. Hay mucho trabajo! he told them, a mock-stern scowl on his face. Work! Get to work! And they scrambled around on the dusty floor giggling, pretending to hammer and saw and measure, things they had seen me do. I want this job *finish!* Slapping the back of one hand against the palm of the other for emphasis. *Now!*

He monitored my daily progress, supervised from the sidewalk while I perched on the roof nailing down new shingles. Good job, lady! he yelled. Soon this house gunna be *finish!* But when I mentioned the possibility of moving in, his face took on a wary expression. You gunna live in *this* house? he asked somberly. No, lady, this house, it's not for you, he said, shaking his head. When I asked him why not, he sighed with exaggerated exasperation, pointing to the empty kitchen as though the proof were self-evident.

Damn, lady, donchoo *see?* There's no *stove*, so how you gunna *cook?*

When school was out for the day, the afternoon half over, Lee and Lonnie and skinny Curtis came dragging up the front walk. The house seemed too small with them in it, sullenly spreading their backpacks and huge puffy coats across the floor. Things fell apart in their hands—springs shot from the orbital sander, hinges snapped, bolts unscrewed themselves and fell through the heater grate. As soon as Alfredo saw them coming, his face changed. Vámonos, he hissed to the little kids, and they all hightailed out the back door.

There were another couple of boys that started coming around the house on Foothill Boulevard. J.J. and Jacy were rivals of Lee and Lonnie and Curtis's. J.J. was short and wide, with large, sleepy eyes and a slow smile jam-packed with teeth. Jacy was tall and slim with small, discreet features, a private distance in his eyes. I called them Triple J. Lee, Lon, and Curtis hated them: they were a little older, bigger and smarter—savvy and entertaining. I liked having them around, I fostered it; as long as they were there the three younger boys stayed away, standing out on the edge of the sidewalk scowling. "And *stay* out!" J.J. yelled, slamming a newly glazed window shut only to fling it open again. "Stupid fucktard *punks!*"

Nemnt drek, macht gelt. That was Mad Dog's philosophy, which I was advised to emulate. Translated from the Yiddish, it meant *Take shit, make gold.* That was the gist of the pep talk he gave me as we lay twined in the bedeviled sheets. It seemed to me sometimes that my situation was more a case of *nemnt gelt, macht drek.* My money was dwindling fast, eaten up, fed into fifty-pound boxes of nails and thundering rolls of asphalt roofing. Graduate school was starting in a month and I wouldn't be there. Instead I was foxholed in a ditch that was collapsing in on itself.

The house was not livable; it might well never be, as far as I could tell. There was no plumbing—all the fixtures had been torn away, leaving mangled pipes. I had to pee in a coffee can. There was no electricity; the tangled jumble of black cords that crisscrossed the attic and snaked down mysteriously between the walls emitted only intermittent flickers accompanied by a scorched metallic smell. The only usable power came through the orange extension cord that stretched across the driveway and under Bert's door, for which I weekly paid him a quixotically determined amount. He took several breaks a day in order to furnish me with another installment in the endless series of overlapping rants regarding the general stupidity of *some people* and their failure to foresee consequences, during one of which I came to know that he had been the one to strip the house of every valuable fixture. "Hey, c'mon, this place has been vacant for ten years!" he said, when he saw my surprise. "Besides, who else around here do you think has the smarts to know the value of an antique claw-foot tub?" He was bragging, a canny light in his eyes. Sometimes his was the only white face I saw for days, and I sensed that the neighborhood felt we were affiliated, that he and I were cut from the same loaf. I came to feel that I hated his face more than I had hated any other human face ever.

But I was dependent on him. That was the truth of it. Most days I didn't know what the fuck I was doing there—it was foolish, dan-gerous beyond belief, why had I thought I could pull off this stunt? Nights I scaled a pyramid of how-to books, cramming for finals in roofing, carpentry, plumbing, and failing every test on these subjects. Alfredo was right; I would never be able to live in this house, I would probably never even be able to finish it. Sometimes I thought my only hope was to try to sell it as-is, as soon as possible, and at least try to recoup my expenses. Bert snorted merrily at this idea. What kind of *idiot* would buy a house like *that*, in a neighborhood like *this*? Blew air through his teeth in sour disgust. The house was more damaged than I ever could have dreamed, the neighborhood was more perilous. I was scared to death on every available level.

In my daydreams, my True Love appeared to rescue me. As I stood transfixed over an unsolvable mess of knob-and-tube wiring he appeared beside me and with a deft hand selected the one specific wire, touched it to another, there was a cheerful spark, and all the lights in the house suddenly glowed with soft incandescence. We hadn't spoken in six months; he didn't know anything about this house, couldn't know anything about what I was doing here. But every time I turned around I expected to see his face.

And then one night I saw him. It was dark outside, pitch black. I had overstayed my welcome, laying down varnish—I was woozy, sick from fumes—and there he was. I couldn't believe my eyes. He had his motorcycle nosed against the curb and was waiting silently for me. He stared intently through the black shadows as I emerged from behind the hinged sheet of plywood that sheathed the dark, deserted house. I let the panel fall and stood to face him. He gasped.

"Lady, you scared the holy shit outta me."

Just some biker dude with a clogged fuel jet. I loaned him a wrench and held the flashlight; his hands were shaking as badly as mine. And then he roared off into the night, looking back with a long, shadow-pocked face.

In the moldy crawl space, digging away at the foundation with my screwdriver, I unearthed the mud-stained head and torso of an antique porcelain doll. Broken toy of some long-dead ghost-child.

She had peach cheeks and a golden bob. Sifting through the old dead dirt I found one perfect leg with a little lick of a black ballet slipper brushed on. I spent a long enough time down there that I guess it got to me that I couldn't find the rest of her. I got it in my head that if I just searched long enough I could restore her, because that began to seem really important to me.

Above my head, the old abandoned house squatted, fretting and moaning. Its many festering grievances needed to be addressed. But I was in the crawl space, playing with dolls. Upstairs, I put her on a high ledge in the kitchen, out of harm's way.

And then she was gone. This was about the time things started to go wrong. Money was missing from my foolproof hiding place; tools had begun disappearing—a mat knife, a crowbar, a cat's paw. Trees I had planted were snapped off at the base, roots ripped up and flung onto the roof. I asked 'Fredo if he'd seen or heard anything; this Alfredo kid, I liked him, I liked everything about him. I didn't know it, of course, but he was a preview of what my own son would someday be. He was eight years old and I trusted him, I wanted his take on the situation; was it, was it *skinny Curtis?* Alfredo stared at me with sparkling, amused eyes. He laughed gaily. *Damn*, lady, donchoo know *nutheen?* His brother said something staccato in Spanish and then they all snickered. Hey lady, my brudda say do you like to eat *chicken?* The merry little faces hung in silence, awaiting, and then they all exploded in laughter, staggering and falling about the place in their tiny, vivid clothing. I was a fool. I was an endless source of amusement to them, a bottomless supply of candy, an opportunity for unprovable, unpunishable hijinks. I suspected all the others knew this, too, everyone in the neighborhood recognized the complete folly of my insane project, knew that I was some variety of raving idiot; and that something was building up. But these kids all wore the same smiling face. I was trapped. I needed them; they were my protection. The day before, the back door had been suddenly yanked from the frame, and one of the local pimps stepped in. He stood with his hands on his hips, breathing hard, surveying me boldly. I stood rooted to the spot, hypnotized: *How could someone do such thing to his teeth, to his two front teeth?* He gave a powerful rolling swivel to his head, took in Alfredo and Diego in the corner dissecting candy bars with the tin snips and meticulously melting them with the soldering iron. Alfredo hit him with a scalding string of invective.

He nodded sagely. All right, he said. Okay. I'll definitely be catching you later, babe. He gave me a menacing, varicolored smile.

That same day Jacy and J.J. helped me drag the huge rusted carcass of the floor furnace out from under the house. It felt like a malignant presence had been banished. We counted to three and heaved it into the bed of my truck, where it hit with shocking, explosive force. And then we stood grinning shyly at each other, elated by our daring, the thunderous commotion we had caused.

Then it was the gray and gritty sheets again. Silt filled the creases of my face, the corners of my eyes, it sifted down from the exposed rafters where Mad Dog had pulled away the old lath and plaster to create a loft. I put both arms up over my face.

A minute later I was up and dressed, sitting in a circle of yellow light, poring over Mad Dog's copy of Richter's *Wiring Simplified*, which tells you everything you need to know about wiring a house, assuming you already know how to do it.

Mad Dog had his long legs stretched out across the bed, his chin pressed into his collarbone. He would let the phlegm collect in his throat at this angle, droning on in a rattly, raspy, gravelly voice, explaining in detail how every single thing in the world worked, and I would listen and wait, and wait, and wait for the terrible voice to wind down, as it did; he let it attenuate, like a gramophone winding down, so it seemed to me that at some point, some time, one of these nights, it had to break down into its component parts, it had to disintegrate into a series of mechanical clicks, a granular series of reports, like a Geiger counter. I wanted to cuff him. I wanted to pitch him violently off the bed. *Clear your throat for God's sake!* I wanted to yell this and other things. But I did not. Because the things he did that annoyed me were *essential*, they were required, they satisfied my sense of injustice; intensified and fed the narcotic suffering I felt I needed to endure in order to be ready. To be worthy of my True Love.

Mad Dog whimpered in his sleep like a crybaby. He mewed like a kitten when he came. However many times I told him not to, he persisted in calling me by a despised diminutive of my name.

How had I ever thought that he would be the one to save me?

Lee and Lonnie couldn't keep their fingers off the newly painted walls. I made them sit inside a chalked circle on the floor while they grazed on candy bars, chewing open-mouthed at each other, displaying terrific stalagmites and stalactites of caramel and nougat. Meanwhile I rolled gigantic Ms and Ws of fresh paint across the water-stained plaster walls; I was discovering that I loved this part, everything afterward clean and new, and I was in the zone, both modulating and answering the rhythmic *bubump thump* of the roller, I was *in the zone*, and then I heard a gush of liquid coming from the closet—the sound of a ruptured pipe where none existed. I yanked the door open and skinny Curtis was in there, his small bird-skull of a head hunched into his shoulders, his hands at his fly, an arc of piss splashing into the corner that I had just painted Almond White.

What the *fuck!* I grabbed his shoulder and spun him around. Piss kept streaming, it jetted across my pant leg, across my shoe, and it kept coming as he continued to rotate until he was facing the back door, and just as the planet of his face swept past mine, the orbs of his eyes swiveled up, showing twin sliver moons at the bottom, and all malignity, all malevolence was gone, there was only shame, and I saw. He couldn't help it. He hadn't known what to do in this house with no toilet, he was just a child, too embarrassed to even ask, and then he was stumbling, running out the back door, plunging down the steps. "Honey," I called, "Curtis—" but he was gone and there was only Lee and Lonnie's hulking laughter.

Maaan, he musta hadda go baaaad.

In the morning I found the remains of the porcelain doll on the back porch, the head crushed, stomped to shards like splinters of white bone, the pointed toe of the shoe shoved lewdly into a leghole.

The whole thing had been doused with lighter fluid in a failed attempt to set it afire. Letters had been scraped into the new wood of the flooring. *We go get you BICH.*

Jacy and J.J. began showing up every afternoon. They helped me unload lumber, ticked through tile samples, passed judgment on paint chips: S'okay, S'lame. S'cool. They built a fort in the vacant lot from the scraps of plywood and sheetrock I gave them and it was solid and good and they were proud of it. Other kids in the neighborhood came by and admired it and I told them this.

Well, these other kids, Jacy wanted to know, were they black or white? Or were they *meskin?* I didn't remember, I'd just seen some kids, I hadn't really noticed, and then it was Naw! *Naw!* Hadn't *noticed?* Because to them everything came down to race, to relative hue, they couldn't see past it, couldn't imagine that anybody else could, ever. *Naw!* And their eyes were big with shame on my behalf, for how could I tell such a colossal fib, how could I say, to them, that I *didn't notice?*

They sucked their lips and shook their heads. Wore pained expressions in every room of the house. Finally decided to shrug it off; did so, elaborately, eloquently, in mime. Forgave me.

Work was getting done. Porcelain fixtures had been ceremonially joined to the house by means of chrome tubes adorned with nuts and washers, the bangles arrayed in the specific ritualistic order that appeased the water gods. Coils of Romex and armored cable spiraled smoothly, balletically, through the walls, replacing the old black wires kinked like spider legs. I let Triple J be the ones to flick the switch when the power was finally restored. They gripped the toggle together, jostling for position, counted to three and pushed, staring up at the fixtures with wondrous excitement as though they had never seen anything like it. I was doing something here.

In every house I've ever owned there was left behind some written trace of the previous occupants, proof of their hectic, harassed lives.

A to-do list, much amended, scratched on the back of a used gas bill, wedged behind the kitchen drawer and lost to scrabbling hands. An angry injunction— *KEEP OUT THIS MEANS YOU!*—printed in furious toppling capitals on the piece of pulpy construction paper that rolled out at me when I levered a jammed pocket door back on track. Jotted digits on a garage wall pertaining to the measurement of some lonesome bit of carpentry, and on a bedroom-closet doorjamb a tentative horizontal stroke fixing the height of R. on 6/1/23. For some reason I saw, while painting cautiously in order to preserve that antique scotch, a buzz-cut adolescent boy craning his skinny neck, lifting his chin ___ _____ to achieve maximum height; a boy who would now, if still living, be an old old man. And what did he remember of that house, that L-shaped bedroom where he slept away his childhood, growing up too fast in his sleep; what did he remember of the hand that made that shy mark, begging time for once to stand still?

In the house on Foothill Boulevard, in a built-in linen cupboard, I found a cylinder of paper rolled snug and poked, by time or purposeful hand, into the gap between wall and shelf; a rudimentary poem in looping, attenuated, feminine scroll in which the writer lamented that her mate was *Drifting Away.* The upper corner was adorned by a belabored depiction of a flower—it was the stricken iris by the back porch that I was trying to coax back to life.

I asked Bert about the people who had owned my house. A couple, he said, childless. Couple of old coots. Died one right after the other in the county hospital, no one to inherit the house.

Had the husband ever left her? Was the man unfaithful?

Bert snorted; *Ray? Ray unfaithful?* Didn't have the guts. Didn't have the blood, a real wetwick. Tied to her apronstrings. No. Nope. They were like this, he said, and ground his hands together in an ugly wriggling mass.

And then Bert stood silent for a moment; the machinery that packed his skull had jammed, temporarily disabled. His small eyes froze in place, and I felt for him. For I had gotten to know this man some little bit. Enough to know that he'd had a love affair, that it had almost destroyed his marriage to the woman he called, even after thirty-nine years, *his bride*—the blue-eyed girl he'd wooed in high school who'd metamorphosed into a hatchet-faced harridan who sat in the locked white Cadillac imperiously blasting the horn in order to summon him from the shop, and he hightailed it, too, his rear tucked under like a scolded dog.

He snapped out of it. "You know, I wonder about you," he said. Standing idly in the driveway with his arms folded, rocking on his heels, gears and pistons whirring again in unison. "Young, good-lookin' gal. And then here comes this crumb-bum with his hand out." Bert had seen me kiss Mad Dog good-bye while stuffing bills into his pocket. I always paid Mad Dog for his time; I didn't want

 that between us. Mad Dog's help cost too much, and I'm not speaking fiscally here.

"Because you know, if he cared about you, you wouldn't be able to keep him away with a stick," Bert said softly, peering hard at the sidewalk.

And that was when I knew. That was when I realized my True Love was never coming back to me. All at once I knew that. There was a feeling like a big clumsy animal thrashing around violently in my chest and I thought I couldn't breathe, I thought my breastbone would split; and then it dropped dead; and there was a taste like ashes in my mouth, like moldy leaves, dirty coins.

In every house I've owned I've left some written trace, a note to the future. In the wedding-cake Victorian where I now live, during the course of some early, optimistic remodeling project that involved precious period wainscotting acquired by special order from an architectural-salvage company in Illinois, I left a note to my son, who was not yet born. A fond *Hello*. If he ever does find it, I'll probably be long dead and gone, and glad of it.

And so too I left a message inside the house on Foothill Boulevard. Nothing fancy. The date and a salutation. Unattributed. Greetings from one possible past.

I was there early on Saturday morning, gathering my tools for the day's project; the house was serene, empty, and I stood idle for a moment enjoying the solitude. And then Curtis materialized in the kitchen with a handgun. I hadn't seen him since the day he flew out the back door. He pulled it out from under his sweater and showed me, holding it awkwardly in his small hands.

I could kill you, he said.

He said it sullenly, disinterestedly, like it would really be too much trouble. But his forehead was jumping, knotted with tension, and he wouldn't look at me.

Whoa, put that away, quick, I said, the way you would to your best pal, the way you would when the teacher looked up just as your friend lifted the lid of his desk to show you the peashooter he had hidden there. I stretched to peep out the window like maybe there was a cop out front, maybe a hundred or so cops, a whole task force, waiting for an excuse to shoot him dead.

Quick, I said, if they see you with that they'll kill you. Put it away. And he did, the thumb-release snagging in the weave of his sweater so that for one long instant he was pressing the muzzle into the soft flesh under his own rib cage and it was all wrong—the bulky, ugly, machine-forged metal against the tender baby skin of his little belly—it was all wrong, it was incongruous, irreconcilable, and then he turned and left, furtively, hunching over.

I should have gone home. The day was tainted; I was rattled, and I should have known no good would come of it. I should have just left. Instead I was out in the backyard mixing concrete in the big pink bucket, setting posts for a fence that would separate the long double yard with its sprawling acacias and copse of birch from the vacant rubble-strewn lots that verged on the avenue, the logjammed river of traffic. This was a gift for Bert in a way, a good-will gesture, for unbelievably, the house was nearing completion. A fence along the south end of his property was something Bert had mentioned longingly—a buffer zone. I was putting it up over the weekend, a surprise for Monday morning. When he saw it he would spit and curse; he would snarl and gripe that it constituted a hazard, that it was just one more place for a burglar to lie in wait, but I didn't know that then, I was on a mission, I was in a rush, there would be barely enough time to finish the wonderful surprise. Triple J came by; they had brought a new kid with them and this kid was white, and this seemed to amuse them somehow. The kid had his dishwater hair stretched back into scrawny cornrows and he had a mean-dog expression like he was continually called on and willing to prove any sort of challenge and they seemed to think maybe this kid and I knew each other, by virtue of our race, or should know each other, and they

 were pleased with themselves, being in the operative position as they were, able to make it happen, they were in high spirits, showing me off, showing him off, showing him to me, me to him, flippant, full of themselves, taunting him, dancing around the acacias, pushing the kid at me. Get it on! We gonna watch while you get it on, blood!

One minute they were horsing around and then Jacy was falling back laughing, pushing off kilter the leveled half-set posts and I got mad, I didn't want to deal with them and I told them to leave, a thing I had never done before, and Jacy stepped up to my face, said Make me and then I was suddenly grappling with him, our hands locked together over our heads, like a game of Mercy, but this was no game. Other boys, attracted by the commotion, began to collect; they formed a loose circle around us and all the customary jeers and taunts were gone and it was dead silent and I was struggling with all my might. *Bad-news bear, you're a bad-news bear*, I was thinking, and, *This is it, this is it.* I was acutely aware of the placement of my tools—my pick, shovel, a small hand sledge I needed to know exactly where each tool was at any given second, that no tool had been picked up, and I was preoccupied with this knowledge as we circled in the dirt. We were face to face, Jacy's jaws and teeth shaking, his spit flying in my face, his pupils silvery and depthless. Jacy was maybe twelve; I had a couple inches on him and in Mercy leverage is everything; I began to feel his knuckles buckle, and I thought if I could hold up I could probably bend him under, and I was thinking, But then what? Then what?

There was a sudden stir, a rushing of centrifugal motion in the periphery, and then kids were scattering, they flew, and Jacy suddenly gave up, went limp, and I turned and saw what they'd seen inching toward us over the broken glass of the vacant lot: a squad car, proceeding almost leisurely to within a couple feet of where my shovel lay. We stood together watching it, heads ducked, breathing hard.

Out popped Officer Cardiac Arrest. Jacy was trying to backpedal slow. The cop barked once, called him back, took down his name. Aw, *maaaan!* Pivoted, took down my name. Wrote us both up in a little black book. Told us how many days he had left on the force before he could retire—3,244—and how he meant to know the names of every single individual who caused him any aggravation whatsoever, how he was going to concentrate all his energy on making life a living hell for those particular individuals. His enunciation was precise and rapid-fire, his delivery entirely convincing. He slapped his book shut and wheeled, fitted himself back into his car while maintaining eye contact. His face was scarlet with congested fury. The window slid down weightlessly and he jerked his head out to snap at me.

"You need to get rid of that house, *now!* You need to get out of this neighborhood, *now!*"

He was already twisted around in his seat, he was already backing out, his window gliding up when I yelled it. *You need to get a coronary bypass, now!*, and Jacy was looking at me with awe, smiling and shaking his head, Man, you *told* him, he was holding his hand out to me, coaching me through a long, elaborate, jiggling handshake—but the cop was already pulling away, his window up snug, and if he even heard me at all it must have sounded like gibberish, like slang, some egregious insult instead of a clinical diagnosis.

The rest is a blur, the time frame telescopes, jams when I try to order it—the coming back to find the house broken into, trashed, words scratched into the beautiful antique rosewood paneling intact up until then; gallons of paint poured on the floor, win-dows shattered, a stack of shit in the sink. There was a trail of footprints, a zigzag pattern of the soles in Almond White, leading out the new back door which had been split, splintered, kicked in. Curtis dragged by on the sidewalk trailing a length of rope, eyes down, and I burned a hole in his back as he turned the corner.

Triple J came by, eyes bright, expressed shock at the damage. Let me see your shoes, I said tonelessly, examining their paintless soles. Okay. Okay. I knew it wasn't you, I said, in apology.

Days later, they came back with their pale friend, lounged on the porch while I replaced the broken panes, but I was not in the mood. I was thinking of the time I saw them crossing at the corner, scrambling to keep up with a woman marching along in black leather boots and a matching jacket, how when I called and waved to them they looked right through me with stony eyes. I remembered an instance weeks before when I'd come upon J.J. crying by the back porch. He was sobbing heartbrokenly, hunched up against the stairs, hugging his knees, and I'd sat down next to him and put my arms around him, murmuring inquiringly, consolingly, whereupon he sprang up, laughing an angry and triumphant laugh. Hah! Gotcha! I *got* you! he cawed. You're a pretty good actor, I'd said, then. I know, he said. Been *practicing*. And here was the taunting again, the insolent, insulting undercurrent—she don't even *know*—thinks she can just *ignore*—like in *her* mind we don't even *egziss!*—fix it, sell it, wham bam thank you ma'am, she's *gone*—what about us? Round your neck with a welfare check, that's what—show *her*. Jacy had on a different pair of shoes now; and when he twisted his foot I saw the zigzag pattern on the sole, and it was packed with Almond White paint and I suddenly rose up, slapping fast their surprised faces, one hard slap each and then they were up, crying, running to the plywood fort in the field and I was there standing alone, shoulders sagging. *Shit.*

What I was looking at now, what I had just touched off, was wall-to-wall retribution; an endless series of escalating attacks.

I trudged to the fort. I called their names. I said I was sorry, and I was. I said I was very sorry and that I hoped that we could still be friends. I said that now we were even. Right? I extended my hand down into the dark. I offered it to shake. I said, Truce, okay? I held it there. Kept holding it out. Finally a small hand reached up, tentatively, and took hold of mine.

I went home and called a succession of realtors until I finally found one desperate enough. I put the house up for sale.

*   *   *

The one thing I would change, the one thing I wish I had done, the thing that wakes me up at 3 a.m.—twisting and writhing in my clean, fresh sheets—is the dog. The dog that Lee and Lonnie's family kept in their basement crawl space. I saw him only once, when he came cringing and groveling out; Lee and Lon were squealing, slapping at the fleas that were jumping off him onto their legs, and Curtis was kicking him viciously back under the house, kept kicking long after the dog had nowhere to go, and I couldn't help it, I rapped on the window, which was covered on the outside with ply-

wood, I slapped at it hard, and instantly Curtis's eyes darted up, and he continued kicking, then stomping, with new vigor, his jaw set, staring up with his weird angry insect eyes to where he knew I was watching through the seam in the plywood. How was it that I had done nothing? Had not called the SPCA, the Humane Society, nothing. I had done nothing. I was scared of my own shadow by then. I was all but gone, and I was scared to death the way Bert was scared to death, scared that in the last frame of the final episode he'd be gunned down, left to die in the dust. I was scared of general repercussions, of course; and specifically on that day I was scared of Lee and Lonnie's father, a man built like a fireplug who had stalked me down the day before, had seemed to chase me in slow motion from one end of the property to the other as I dragged a rotted concrete-encased post from the back of the lot to my truck, in order to tell me that I was never, never to tell his boys what they should and shouldn't do again. *Never!* Wasn't none of my business. *His* business and I was to stay out of it! Red eyes and a white web of saliva at the corners of his mouth.

What I had told his boys was that if they ever saw Curtis with a gun they should try to get away from him as quickly as they could.

Curtis was killed that summer. Not by way of a gun. He was hit by a car on Foothill Boulevard. Alfredo told me. Hey, lady, he said, guess what. Curtis had been chasing his cat. Or he was chasing a cat, a different thing. There is that in me that wants it to have been a certain way: his intention to harm the cat, not rescue it, so that there might be some logic in his death; so it could be seen as the merciful interruption of a pattern of violence that would come to no good end.

Mad Dog and I had been boxing on the day the call came. A guy had shown up with the asking price in hundred-dollar bills in a shoe-box. Looking back, it doesn't seem like that much money. But it was enough to fuel the small real-estate empire that would consume and sustain me over the next decades. According to the realtor the guy was buying the house for his mother; according to Bert, he was a drug dealer who wanted the house, with its central location, for distribution purposes. I see no reason in the world as I now know it why both versions cannot be absolutely true and cor-rect. But I don't know; I never went back.

Earlier on that day, I had laced a pair of boxing gloves onto Mad Dog's big hands, and then worked my own pair on. My True Love had taught me to spar, it was something we had liked to do together, and while we were scrapping he would praise my grace and exceptional reflexes, meanwhile delivering, out of nowhere, a series of invisibly arriving, playful taps to my shoulder.

Mad Dog stood up, and I circled him, feinting lightly. I socked him softly on the shoulder and he flinched; and just as I turned away he lifted his glove and swung, tagging me on the jaw with a round-house punch. So that later, when the call from the realtor came, I had the type of splitting headache that gives you a view of exploding stars as you lean over to throw up, and which, since it heralded an end to my involvement with Foothill Boulevard and with Mad Dog, I have ever since associated with good luck and hope and prosperity.

RETREAT

by WELLS TOWER

(A different version of this story originally appeared in McSweeney's 23. For a note about its return, please see this issue's copyright page.)

Sometimes, after six or so large drinks, it seems like a sane idea to call my little brother on the phone. Approximately since Stephen's birth, I've held him among the principal motherfuckers of my life, and it takes a lot of solvent to bleach out all the dark recollections I've stashed up over the years. Pick a memory, any memory. My eleventh birthday party at Ernstead Park, how about? I'd just transferred schools, trying to turn over a new leaf, and I'd invited all the boys and girls of quality. I'd been making progress with them, too, until Stephen, age eight, ran up behind me at the fish pond and shoved me face-first into the murk. The water came up only to my knees, so I did a few hilarious staggers before flopping down, spluttering, amid some startled koi. The kids all laughed like wolves.

Or ninth grade, when I caught the acting bug and landed a part in our high school's production of *Grease* playing opposite a girl named Dodi Clark. We played an anonymous prancing couple, on stage only for the full-cast dance melees. She was no beauty, a mousy girl with a weak chin and a set of bonus, overlapping canine teeth, but I liked her somewhat. She had a pretty neat set of breasts for a girl her age. I thought maybe we could help each other out with our virginity problems. Yet the sight of Dodi and me dancing drove Stephen into a jealous fever. Before I could get my angle going, Stephen snaked me, courting her with a siege of posters, special pens, stickers, and crystal whim-whams. The onslaught worked and Dodi fell for him, but when she finally parted her troubled mouth to kiss him, he told me years later, he froze up. "I think I had some kind of primeval prey-versus-predator response when I saw those teeth. It was like trying to make out with a sand shark. No idea why I was after her to begin with."

But I know why: in Stephen's understanding, nothing pleasant should ever flow to me on which he hasn't exercised first dibs. He wouldn't let me eat a turd without first insisting on his cut.

He's got his beefs, too, I suppose. I used to tease him pretty rigorously. We had these little red toads that hopped around my mother's yard, and I used to pin him down and rub them into his clenched teeth. Once, when we were smoking dope in high school, I lit his hair on fire. Another time, I locked him outside for in his underwear until the snot froze in scales on his face. Hard to explain why I did these things, except to say that I've got a little imp inside me whose ambrosia is my brother's wrath. Stephen's furies are marvelous, ecstatic, somehow pornographic, the equally transfixing inverse of watching people in the love act. That day I locked him out, I was still laughing when I let him in after a cold hour. I even had a mug of hot chocolate ready for him. He drained it and then grabbed a can opener from the counter and threw it at me, gouging a three-inch gash beneath my lower lip. It left a white parenthesis in the stubble of my chin, the abiding, sideways smile of the imp.

*   *   *

But give me a good deep rinse of alcohol and our knotty history unkinks itself. All of the old crap seems inconsequential, just part of the standard fraternal rough-and-tumble, and I get very soppy and bereft over the brotherhood Steve and I have lost.

Anyhow, I started feeling that way one night in October just after I'd crossed the halfway point on a fifth of Meyer's rum. I was standing at the summit of a small mountain I'd recently bought in Aroostook County, Maine. The air was wonderful, heavy with the watery sweetness of lupine, moss, and fern. Overhead, bats hawked mosquitoes in the darkening sky, while the sun waned behind the molars of the Appalachian range. I browsed the contacts on my phone, wanting to call someone up, maybe just deliver an oral post-card of this place into someone's voicemail box, but I had a reason not to dial each of those names until I got to Stephen's.

I dialed, and he answered without saying hello.

"In a session," he said, the last syllable trilling up in a bitchy way, and hung up the phone. Stephen makes his living as a music thera-pist, but session or not, you'd think he could spare a second to at least say hello to me. We hadn't spoken in eight months. I dialed again.

"What the fuck, fool, it's Matthew."

"Matthew," he repeated, in the way you might say "cancer" after the doctor's diagnosis. "I'm with a client. This is not an optimum time."

"Yeah," I said. "Question for you: mountains."

There was a wary pause. From Stephen's end came the sound of someone doing violence to a tambourine.

"What about them?"

"Do you like them? Do you like mountains, Stephen?"

"I have no objection to them. Why?"

"Well, I bought one," I said. "I'm on it now."

"Congratulations," Stephen said. "Is it Popacateptl? Are you putting 7-Elevens on the Matterhorn?"

Over the years, I've made a hell of a lot of money in real estate, and this seems to hurt Stephen's feelings. He's not a church man, but he's big on piety and sacrifice and letting you know what choice values he's got. So far as I can tell, his values include eating ramen noodles by the case, getting laid once every fifteen years or so, and arching his back at the sight of people like me—that is, people who have amounted to something and don't reek of thrift stores.

But I love Stephen. Or I think I do. We've had some intervals of mutual regard. Our father came down with lymphoma when Stephen was four, so we pretty much parented ourselves while our mother nursed our father through two exhausting cycles of remission and relapse.

At any rate, the cancer got our father when I was ten. Liquor killed our mother before I was out of college, and it was right around then that we went on different courses. Stephen, a pianist, retreated into a bitter fantasy of musical celebrity that was perpetually being thwarted—by his professors at the Eastman School, by the philistines in his ensembles, and by girlfriends who wanted too much of his time. He had a series of tedious artistic crackups, and whenever we'd get together, he'd hand me lots of shit about how drab and hollow my life was.

Actually, my life was extremely full. I married young, and married often. I bought my first piece of property at eighteen. Now, at forty-two, I've been through two amicable divorces. I've lived and made money in nine American cities. Late at night, when rest won't come and my breathing shortens with the worry that I've cheated myself of life's traditional rewards (long closenesses, offspring, mature plantings), I take an astral cruise of the hundreds of properties that have passed through my hands over the years, and before I come close to visiting them all, I droop, contented, into sleep.

When no orchestras called Stephen with commissions, he exiled himself to Eugene, Oregon to buff his oeuvre while eking out a living teaching the mentally substandard to achieve sanity by blowing on harmonicas. When I drove down to see him two years ago after a conference in Seattle, I found him living above a candle store in a dingy apartment which he shared with a dying collie. The animal was so old it couldn't take a leak on its own, so Stephen was always having to lug her downstairs to the grassy verge beside the sidewalk. Then he'd straddle the dog and manually void its bladder via a Heimlich technique horrible to witness. You hated to see your last blood relation engaged in something like that. I told Stephen that from a business standpoint, the smart thing would be to have the dog put down. This caused an ugly argument, but really, it seemed to me that someone regularly seen by the roadside hand-juicing a half-dead dog was not the man you'd flock to for lessons on how to be less out of your mind.

"The mountain doesn't have a name yet," I told him. "Hell, I'll name it after you. I'll call it Brown Cloud Hill"—my old nickname for the gloomy man.

"Do that," said Stephen. "Hanging up now."

"I send you any pictures of my cabin? Gets its power off a wind-mill. I'm telling you, it's the absolute goddamned shit. You need to come out here and see me."

"What about Charleston? Where's Amanda?"

I spat a lime rind into my hand and tossed it up at the bats to see if they'd take a nibble at it. They didn't.

"No idea."

"You split?"

"Right."

"Oh, jeez, big brother. Really? Wedding's off?"

"Yep."

"What happened? "

"Got sick of her, I guess."

"Why?"

"She was hard of hearing and her pussy stank."

"That's grand. Now look—"

Actually, like about fifty million other Americans, I'd been blind-sided by sudden reverses in the real-estate market. I'd had to borrow some cash from my ex-fiancée, Amanda, an Oldsmobile dealership heiress who didn't care about money just so long as she didn't have to loan out any of hers. Strains developed and the engagement withered. I used the last of my liquidity to buy my hill. Four hundred acres, plus a cabin, nearly complete, thanks to my good neighbor George Tabbard, who'd also cut me a bargain on the land. The shit of it was I'd have to spend a year up in residence here, but I could deal with that. Next fall I could subdivide, sell the plots, dodge the extortionary tax assessment the state charges non-resident speculators, and float into life's next phase with the winds of increase plumping my sails and a vacation home in the deal.

"Anyway," I went on. "Here's a concept. Pry the flute out of your ass and come see me. We'll have real fun. Come now. I'll be under a glacier in six weeks."

"And get the airfare how? Knit it? Listen, I've got to go."

"Fuck the airfare," I told him. "I'll get it. Come see me." It wasn't an offer I really wanted to make. Stephen probably had more money in the bank than I did, but his poor-mouthing worked an irksome magic on me. I couldn't take a second of it without wanting to smack him in the face with a roll of doubloons. Then he said he couldn't leave Beatrice (the collie was still alive!). Fine, I told him, if he could find the right sort of iron lung to stable her in, I'd foot the bill for that too. He said he'd think it over. A marimba flourish swelled on the line, and I let Stephen go.

The conversation left me feeling irritable, and I walked back to my cabin in a low mood. But I bucked up right away when I found George Tabbard on my porch, half of which was still bare joists. He was standing on a ladder, nailing a new piece of trim across the front gable. "Evening, sweetheart," George called out to me. "Whipped up another *objet* for you here."

George was seventy-six, with a head of scraggly white hair. His front teeth were attached to a partial plate that made his gums itch so he didn't wear it, and his breath was like a ripe morgue. At this point, George was basically my best friend, a turn I couldn't have imagined ten months ago when life was still high. His family went back in the area two centuries or so, but he'd moved around a good deal, gone through some wives and degrees and left some children here and there before moving back a decade ago. He'd pretty much built my cabin himself for ten dollars an hour. He was good company. He liked to laugh and drink and talk about road grading, women, and maintaining equipment. We'd murdered many evenings that way.

A couple of groans with his screw gun and he'd secured the item, a four-foot battery of little wooden pom-poms, like you'd see dangling from the ceiling of a Mexican drug dealer's sedan. I'd praised the first one he'd made, but now George had tacked his lacework fancies to every eave and soffit in sight, so that the house pretty well foamed with them. An otherwise sensible person, he seemed to fear a demon would take him if production slowed, and he slapped up a new piece of frippery about every third day. My house was starting to resemble something you'd buy your mistress to wear for a weekend in a cheap motel.

"There we are," he said, backing away to get the effect. "Pretty handsome booger, don't you think?"

"Phenomenal," I said.

"Now how about some backgammon?"

 I went inside and fetched the set, the rum, and a jar of olives. George was a brutal prodigy, and the games were dull routs, yet we sat for many hours in the cool of the evening, drinking rum, moving the lacquered discs around the board, and spitting olive pits over the rail, where they landed quietly in the dark.

To my surprise, Stephen called me back. He said he'd like to come, so we fixed a date, two weeks later. It was an hour and twenty minutes to the village of Aiden, where the airfield was. When George and I arrived, Stephen's plane hadn't come in. I went into the Quonset hut they use for a terminal. A little woman with a brown bomber jacket and a bulb of gray hair sat by the radio, reading the local newspaper.

"My brother's flight was due in from Bangor at eleven," I told the woman.

"Plane's not here," she said.

"I see. Do you know where it is?"

"Bangor."

"And when's it going to arrive?"

"If I knew that, I'd be somewhere picking horses, wouldn't I?"

Then she turned back to her newspaper and brought our chat to an end. The front-page story of the Aroostook *Gazette* showed a photograph of a dead chow dog, under the headline, "Mystery Animal Found Dead in Pinemont."

"Quite a mystery," I said. "The Case of What Is Obviously a Dog."

"'Undetermined origin,' says here."

"It's a dog, a chow," I said.

"Undetermined," the woman said.

With time to kill, we went over the lumberyard in Aiden and I filled the bed of my truck with a load of decking to finish the porch. Then we went back to the airfield. Still no plane. George tried to hide his irritation, but I knew he wasn't happy to be stuck on this errand. He wanted to be out in the woods, gunning for deer. George was keen to get one before the weather made hunting a misery. Loading your freezer with meat slain by your hand was evidently an unshirkable autumn rite around here, and George and I had been going out about every fourth day since the opener three weeks ago. I'd shot the head off a bony goose at point-blank range, but other than that, we hadn't hit a thing. When I'd suggested that we go in on a side of beef from the butcher shop, George had acted as though I'd proposed a terrible breach of code. Fresh venison tasted better than store-bought beef, he argued. Also you were not out big money in the common event that your freezer was sacked by the meat burglars who worked the outer county.

To buck George up, I bought him lunch at a tavern in Aiden, where we ate hamburgers and drank three whiskey sours each. George sighed a lot and didn't talk. Already, I felt a coursing anger at Stephen for not calling to let me know that his plane was delayed. I was brooding heavily when the bartender asked if I wanted anything else. I told him, "Yeah, tequila and cream."

"You mean a Kahlúa and cream," he said, which was what I'd meant, but I wasn't in a mood to be corrected.

"How about you bring what I ordered?" I told him, and he got to work. The drink was bilious, vile, but I forced it down. The bartender told me, sneering, that I was welcome to another, on the house.

When we rolled back by the airport, the plane had come and gone. A light rain was sifting down. Stephen was out by the gate, on the lip of a drainage gully, perched atop his luggage with his chin on his fist. He was thinner than when I'd last seen him, and the orbits of his eyes were dark, kind of buttholish with exhaustion. The rain had wet him through, and what was left of his hair lay sad against his skull. His coat and pants were huge on him. The wind gusted and Stephen billowed like a poorly tarped load.

"Hi, friend!" I called out to him.

"What the shit, Matthew?" he said. "I just stayed up all night on a plane to spend two hours sitting in a ditch? That really happened?"

Of course, Stephen could have waited with the radio woman in the Quonset hut, but he'd probably arranged himself in the ditch to present a picture of maximum misery when I pulled up.

"You could have let me know you got hung up in Bangor. I shit-canned three hours waiting for you. We had stuff on our plate, but now George is drunk and I'm half in the bag and the whole day's shot. Frankly, I'm a little heated at you here."

Stephen bulged his eyes at me. His fists clenched and un-clenched very quickly. He looked about to thrombose. "Extraordinary! This is my fault now? Oh, you are a remarkable prick. This is your fucking... region, Matthew. It didn't occur to me that you'd need to be coached on how not to leave some-body in the rain. Plus call you how, shitball? You know I don't do cell phones."

"Come get in the truck."

I reached for him and he tore his arm away.

"No. Apologize to me." He was red-eyed and shivering. His cheeks and forehead were welted over from repeated gorings by the vicious cold-weather mosquitoes they had up here. Right now, one was gorging itself on the rim of his ear, its belly glowing like a pomegranate seed in the cool white sun. I didn't swat it away for him.

"Mother*fucker*, man. Just get in the truck."

"Forget it. I'm going home." He shouldered his bag and stormed off for the airfield. His tiny damp head, and squelching shoes—it was like watching the tantrum of a stray duckling.

Laughing, I jogged up behind Stephen and stripped the bag from his shoulder. When he turned I put him in a bear hug and kissed his brow.

"Get off me, you ape," he said.

"Who's a furious fellow?" I said. "Who's my little Brown Cloud?"

"Fucking asshole, I'll bite you, I swear," he said into my chest. "Let me go. Give me my bag."

"Ridiculous," I said.

I walked to the truck and levered the seat forward to usher Stephen into the club cab's rear compartment. When Stephen saw that we weren't alone, he stopped grasping for his bag and making departure threats. I introduced Stephen to George. Then my brother clambered in and we pulled onto the road.

"This is Granddad's gun, isn't it?" said Stephen. Hanging in the rack was the .300 Weatherby magnum I'd collected from my grandfather's house years ago. It was a beautiful instrument, with a blued barrel and a tiger-maple stock.

"Yes," I said, marshalling a defense for why I hadn't offered the gun to Stephen, who probably hadn't fired a rifle in fifteen years. Actually, Stephen probably had a stronger claim to it than I did. As kids, we'd gone out for ducks and rabbits with our grandfather, and Stephen, without making much of it, had always been the more patient stalker and a better shot. But he did not mention it.

"Hey, by the way," he said. "The tab comes to eight-eighty."

"What tab?" I said.

"Eight hundred and eighty dollars," Stephen said. "That's what the flight came to, plus a sitter for Beatrice."

"Your daughter?" George asked.

"Dog," said Stephen.

"George, this is a dog that knows where it was when JFK was shot," I said. "Stephen, are you still doing those bowel lavages on her? Actually, don't tell me. I don't need the picture in my head."

"I'd like my money," Stephen said. "You said you'd reimburse me."

"Don't get a rod-on about it, Steve-O. You'll get paid."

"Lovely. When?"

"At some future fucking juncture when I don't happen to be operating a moving motor vehicle. Is that okay with you?"

"Sure," said Stephen. "But just for the record, me being colossally shafted is how this is going to conclude."

"You little grasping fuck, what do you want, collateral? Want to hold my watch?" I joggled the wheel a little. "Or maybe I'll just drive this truck into a fucking tree. Maybe you'd like that."

George began to laugh in a musical wheeze. "How about you stop the car and you two have yourselves an old-fashioned rock fight."

"We're fine," I said, my face hot. "Sorry, George."

"Forget it," Stephen said.

"Oh, no, Steve, money man, let's get you squared away," I said. "George, my checkbook's in the glove box."

George made out the check, and I signed it, which hurt me deeply. I passed it to my brother, who folded it into his pocket.

George patted my shoulder. "His name shall be called Wonderful Counselor, the Everlasting Father, the Prince of Peace," he said.

"Oh, suck a dong," I said.

"If there's no way around it," sighed George. "How's clearance under that steering wheel?"

"Fairly snug."

"A little later, how about, when I can really put my back into it?"

"That's a big ten-four," I said.

At all this, Stephen tittered. Then, after being such a childish shit about the check, he began a campaign of being very enthusiastic about everything going past the windows of the truck. The junky houses with appliances piled on their porches? "Refreshing" compared with the "twee fraudulence of most New England towns." Two hicks on a four-wheeler, blasting again and again through their own gales of dust, knew "how to do a weekend right." "Wagnerian" is how he described the storm clouds overhead. Then Stephen began plying George with a barrage of light and pleasant chatter. Had he lived here long? Ten years? Amazing! He'd grown up here, too? How fantastic to have escaped a childhood in the exurban soul vacuum we'd been reared in. And George had gone to Syracuse? Had he heard of Nils Aughterard, the music biographer on the faculty there? Well, his book on Gershwin—

"Hey, Stephen," I broke in. "You haven't said anything about my new truck."

"What'd you pay for it?"

"Best vehicle I've ever owned," I said. "V-8, five liter. Three-and-a-half-ton towing capacity. Carriage-welded, class-four trailer hitch. Four-wheel drive, max payload package. It'll pay for itself when the snow hits."

"So you and Amanda, that's really off?"

"Yeah."

"I'm so sorry, Matty," Stephen said. "You were so hot on her."

Stephen had despised her. Amanda was a churchgoer, and a Republican. They'd argued about the war in Iraq. Over dinner, Stephen had baited her into declaring that she'd like to see the Middle East bombed to a parking lot. He'd asked her how this tactic would square with "Thou Shalt Not Kill." She'd told him "Thou Shalt Not Kill" was from the Old Testament, so it didn't really count.

"Anyway, I'm sorry," he went on. "I know it's got to hurt."

I took a tube of sunflower seeds from the dashboard and shook a long gray dose into my mouth.

"To be honest with you," I said, cracking a seed with my back teeth. "I just don't see the rationale for anybody owning a vehicle without a carriage-welded, class-four trailer hitch."

In silence, we rode through bleary, rural abridgements of towns, down a narrowing vasculature of country roads, to the rilled and cratered fire trail that served as a driveway to my and George's land. High weeds stood in the spine of earth between the tire grooves, brushing the truck's undercarriage with a sound of light sleet. We passed George's handsome cedar-shake cottage, I dropped the truck into four-wheel drive, and the Dodge leapt, growling, up the hill.

My home hove into view. I was ready for Stephen to bust my balls a little over George's fancy trim, but he took in the place without a word.

George ambled off to take a leak in the trees. I grabbed Stephen's bag and led him indoors. Though my cabin's exterior was well into its late Rococo phase, the interior was still raw. Stephen gazed around the living room. I felt newly conscious of the squalor of the place. The floors were still dusty plywood. The drywall stopped four feet from the floor, and pink insulation lay like an autopsy specimen behind the cloudy plastic sheeting. The sheetless mattress I'd been sleeping on sat askew in the center of the room.

"Feel free to do a little embellishing when you send out the Christmas letter this year," I told him.

Stephen went to the window and gazed out at the wiry expanse of leafless trees sloping down the basin of the valley. "Hell of a view," he said. Then he turned away from the window and looked at the mattress. "You got a place for me to sleep?"

I nodded at a sleeping pad rolled up in the corner. "Top-of-the-line pad, right there. Ever get down on memory foam?"

"You didn't tell me we'd be camping."

"Yeah, well, if it's too much of a shithole for you, baby brother, I can run you back to the motor lodge in Aiden."

"Of course not," Stephen said. "The place is great. I think you're making real progress, Matthew. Honestly, I was expecting a modular chalet with tiered Jacuzzis and an eight-car garage."

"Next time you visit, I'll strip nude and wear a barrel, maybe get a case of hookworm going," I said. "You'll really be proud of me then."

"No, I'm serious. I'd kill for something like this," he said, reaching up to rub his hand along a smooth log rafter. "I mean, God, next month I'm forty. I rent a two-room apartment full of silverfish and no bathroom sink."

"That same place? You're kidding," I said. "What about that condo you were looking at?"

"Cold feet, I guess, with the economy and all. I figured I'd just get rooked."

"It's still on the market? You should've called me. I'd get you set up."

"No."

"But that money, your Gram-Gram cash? Still got it for a down payment?"

He nodded.

"Listen, you get back to Oregon, we'll find you something. Look around, send me some comps, I'll help you through it. We'll get you into a place."

Stephen gave me a guarded look, as though I'd offered him a soda and he wasn't sure I hadn't pissed in it first.

I wanted to get the porch wrapped up before dark, and I suggested that Stephen take a drink up to the summit, where I'd hung a hammock, while George and I nailed the decking down. Stephen said, "Why don't I help you guys? I'm acquainted with Manuel."

"Who?"

"Manuel Labòr," he said, and giggled.

So we unloaded the wood and he and George got to work while I stayed inside, slathering auburn Minwax on sheets of beadboard wainscot. Whenever I poked my head out the front door, I saw Stephen vandalizing my lumber. He'd bend every third nail, and then gouge the wood with the hammer's claw trying to correct his mistake. Water would pool in those gouges and rot the boards, but he seemed to be enjoying himself. Through the closed windows, I could hear George and Stephen chatting and laughing as they worked. I'd learned to tolerate long hours of silence in the months I'd been up here, to appreciate it, even. But it warmed me to hear voices coming from my porch, though in the back of my mind I suspected they were laughing about me.

George and Stephen took until nightfall to get all the decking in place. When they were finished, we made our way down to the tiny pond I'd built by damming a spring behind my house. We shed our clothes and pushed off into the pond, each on his own gasping course through the exhilarating blackness of the water. "Oh, oh, oh, *God* it feels good," cried Stephen in a voice of such carnal gratitude that I pitied him. But it was glorious, the sky and the water of a single world-ending darkness, and we levitated in it until we were as numb as the dead.

Back at the house, I cooked up a gallon or so of beef stroganoff, seasoned as George liked it, with enough salt to make you weep. A run of warm nights was upon us, thanks to a benevolent spasm of the Gulf Stream, and we dined in comfort on the newly finished porch. Over the course of the meal, we put away three bottles of wine and half a handle of gin. By the time we'd moved on to brandied coffee to go with the blueberry pie George fetched from his place, the porch was humid with bonhomie.

"Look at this," Stephen said, stomping heavily on one of the new boards. "Man, I put this bastard here. Some satisfying shit. God bless 'em, there's 'tards I've worked with ten years and we still haven't gotten past chants and toning. But look—" he clogged again on the board. "Couple hours with a hammer. Got something you can stand on. I ought to do like you, Matty. Come out here. Build me a spot."

"Hell yeah, you should," I said. "By the way, how big's that wad you've got? What's it, twenty grand or something?"

"I guess," he said.

"Because look, check it out," I said. "Got a proposition for you. Listen, how many guys like us do you think there are out there? Ballpark figure."

"What's that mean, 'like us'?" Stephen said.

Then I began to spell out for him an idea I'd had on my mind lately, one that seemed rosiest after a wine-soaked dinner, when my gladness for the land, the stars, and the bullfrogs in my pond was at its maximum. I'd get to thinking about the paunchy hordes, nightly pacing carpeted apartments from Spokane to Chattanooga, desperate for an escape hatch. The plan was simple. I'd advertise one-acre plots in the back pages of men's magazines, put up a few spec cabins, handle the contracting myself, build a rifle range, some snow-mobile trails, maybe a little saloon on the summit. In they'd swarm, a hill of pals, a couple of million in it for me, no sweat!

"I don't know," said Stephen, helping himself to another fat dollop of brandy.

"What don't you know?" I asked him. "That twenty grand, you're in for an even share. You'd be getting what the other investors are getting for fifty."

"What other investors?" Stephen asked.

"Ray Lawton," I lied. "Lawton, Ed Hayes, and Dan Welsh. My point is I could let you in, even just with that twenty. If you could kick that twenty in, I'd set you up with an even share."

"No, yeah, I like it," Stephen said. "It's just I need to be careful with that money. That's my whole savings and everything."

"Now goddammit, Stephen, I'm sorry but let me explain something to you. I *make* money, that's what I do," I said. "I take land, and a little bit of money, and then I turn it into lots of money. You follow me? That's what I do. What I'm asking is to basically just *hold* your cash for five months, max, and in return you'll be in on something that, guaranteed, will change your life."

"Can't do it," he said.

"Okay, Stephen, what can you do? Could you go ten? Ten grand for a full share? Could you put in ten?"

"Look, Matthew—"

"Five? Three? Two thousand?"

"Look—"

"How about eight hundred, Stephen, or two hundred? Would that work for you, or would two hundred dollars break the bank?"

"Two hundred's good," he said. "Put me down for that."

"Go fuck yourself," I said.

"Matthew, come on," said George. "Cool it. "

"I'm totally cool," I said.

"No, you're being a shit," said George. "And anyway, your dude ranch thing isn't worth all this gas. Never work."

"Why not?"

"First of all, the county'd never let you do it in the watershed. The ten-acre buffer—"

"I already talked to them about a variance," I said. "Wouldn't be—"

"And for another thing, I didn't move back here to get among a bunch of swinging dicks."

"Due respect, George, I'm not talking about your land."

"I know that, Matthew," George said. "What I'm saying is, you carve this hill up and sell it out to a bunch of cock-knockers from Boston, I'd say the chance is pretty good that some night in the off-season, I'd get a few too many beers in me and I'd get it in my head to come around with a few gallons of kerosene."

George was staring at me with an irritating, stagy intensity. "Forget the kerosene, George—a hammer and nails'll do it," I said, turning and sweeping a hand at the wooden dainties on my gable. "Just sneak up some night and do a little raid with your scrollsaw. Turn everybody's camp into a huge doily. That'll run them off pretty quick."

I laughed and went on laughing until my stomach muscles ached and tears beaded on my jaw. When I looked back at George, he had his lips set in a taut little dash. He was evidently vain about his scrollsaw work. I was still holding my pie plate, and without giving it much thought, I flung it into the woods. A crash followed, but no rewarding tinkle of shattered crockery.

"Ah, fuck," I said.

"What?" said Stephen.

"Nothing," I said. "My life is on fire."

Then I went into my cabin and got down on my mattress, and before long I was sleeping very well.

I woke a little after three, hungover and thirsty as a poisoned rat, but I lay paralyzed in superstition that staggering to the sink would banish sleep for good. My heart raced. I thought of my performance on the porch, then of a good thick noose creaking as it swung. I thought of Amanda, and my two ex-wives. I thought of my first car whose engine seized because I didn't change the timing belt at 100,000 miles. I thought of how two nights ago I'd lost thirty dollars to George in a cribbage game. I thought of how in the aftermath of my father's death, for reasons I couldn't recall, I stopped wearing underwear, and of a day in junior high when the cold rivet in a chair alerted me to a hole in the seat of my pants. I thought of everyone I owed money to, and everyone who owed me money. I thought of Stephen and me and the children we'd so far failed to produce, and how in the diminishing likelihood that I did find someone to smuggle my genetic material into, by the time our little one could tie his shoes, his father would be a florid fifty-year-old who would suck the innocence and joy from his child as greedily as a desert wanderer savaging a found orange.

I wanted the sun to rise, to make coffee, to get out in the woods with George and find his trophy buck, to get back to spinning the blanket of mindless incident that was doing an ever-poorer job of masking the pit of regrets I found myself peering into most sleepless nights. But the sun was slow in coming. The montage wore on until dawn, behind it the soothing music of the noose, *crik-creak, crik-creak, crik-creak.*

At the first bruised light in the eastern windows, I got up. The air in the cabin was dense with chill. Stephen wasn't on the spare mattress. I put on my boots, jeans, and a canvas parka, filled a thermos with hot coffee, and drove the quarter mile to George's house.

The lights were on at George's. George was doing sit-ups and Stephen was at the counter, minting waffles. A very cozy pair. The percolator was gasping away, making me feel forlorn with my plaid thermos.

"Hey, hey," I said.

"There he is," Stephen said. He explained that he'd slept on George's couch. They'd been up late at the backgammon board. He handed me a waffle, all cheer and magnanimity, on his way toward another social heist in the Dodi Clark vein.

"What do you say, George," I said, when the old man had finished his crunches. "Feel like going shooting?"

"I suppose," he said. He turned to Stephen. "Coming with, little brother?"

"I don't have a gun for him," I said.

"Got that .30-.30 he can use," George said.

"Why not?" said Stephen.

Our spot was on Pigeon Lake, twenty miles away, and you had to boat out to the evergreen cover on the far shore. After breakfast, we hooked George's skiff and trailer to my truck, and went jouncing into the white fog that blanketed the road.

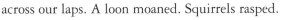

We dropped the boat into the water. With Stephen in the bow, I took the stern. We went north, past realms of marsh grass and humps of pink granite, which, in the hard red light of morning, resembled corned beef hash.

George stopped the boat at a stretch of muddy beach where he said he'd had some luck before. We beached the skiff, and trudged into the tree line.

My calamitous hangover was worsening. I felt damp, unclean, and suicidal, and couldn't concentrate on anything except the vision of a cool, smooth-sheeted bed and iced seltzer water and bitters. It was Stephen who found the first heap of deer sign, in the shadow of a pine sapling stripped orange by a rutting buck. He was thrilled with his discovery, and he scooped the droppings into his palm and carried them over to George, who sniffed the dark pebbles so avidly that for a second I thought he might eat them.

"Pretty fresh," said Stephen, who hadn't been out hunting since the eleventh grade.

George said, "Looks like he winded us. Good eyes, Steve."

"Yeah, I just looked down and there it was," said Stephen.

George went off to perch in a nearby stand he knew about and left the two of us alone. Stephen and I sat at adjacent trees with our guns across our laps. A loon moaned. Squirrels rasped.

"So Matty, you kind of put a weird bug in my ear last night."

"That a fact?"

"Not that ridiculous bachelor-campus thing. But this place is fantastic. George said he sold it to you for ninety bucks an acre. Is that true?"

"Market price," I said.

"Astounding."

"You'd hate it out here. What about your work?"

"I'd just come out here for the summers when my gig at the school slacks off. I need to get out of Eugene. It's destroying me. I don't go out. I don't meet people. I sit in my apartment, composing this crap. I'm done. I could have spent the last two decades shooting heroin and the result would be the same, except I'd have some actual life behind me."

I lifted a haunch to let a long, low fart escape.

"Charming," said Stephen. "How about you sell me two acres? Then I've got twelve thousand to put into a cabin."

"I thought you had twenty."

"I *had* twenty-three," he said. "Now I've got about twelve."

"You spent it? On what?"

"Investments," he said. "Some went to this other thing."

"What other thing?"

Distractedly, he pinched a few hairs from his brow. I watched him put the hairs into his mouth and nibble them rapidly with his front teeth. "I've got a thing with this girl."

"Hey, fantastic," I said. "You should have brought her. What's her name?"

"Luda," Stephen said. "She's Hungarian."

"Far fucking out," I said. "What's a Hungarian chick doing in Eugene?"

"She's still in Budapest, actually," Stephen said. "We're trying to get the distance piece of it ironed out."

"How'd you meet her?"

"That's sort of the weird part. I met her online."

"Nothing wrong with that."

Stephen coughed and ripped another sprig from his brow. "Yeah, but, I mean, it was one of these things. To be totally honest, I met her on this site. Really, pretty tame stuff. I mean, she wasn't, like, fucking people or anything. It was just, you know, you pay a few bucks and you can chat with her, and she's got this video feed."

I looked at him to see if he was kidding. His face was grim and earnest. "You and like fifty other guys, right?" I said after a while.

"No, no. Well, yeah," Stephen said. "I mean, there is a group room or whatever, but if you want to, you can, like, do a private thing where it shuts out all the other subscribers and it's just the two of you. And over time, we started really getting to know each other. Every once in a while, I'd log in under a different name, you know, to see how she'd act with other guys, and almost every time she guessed it was me! A few months ago, I set up a camera so she could see me, too. A lot of the time, we don't even do anything sexual. We just talk. We just share our lives with each other, just stuff that happens in our day."

"But you pay her, Stephen," I said.

"Not always," he said. "Not anymore. She's not a whore. She's really just a normal woman. She's getting her degree in computer science. She's got a little son, Miska. I've met him, too. But, yeah, I try to help them when I can. I ought to show you some of her emails. She's very smart. A good writer. She's probably read more books than I have. It's not as weird as it sounds, Matty. We're talking about me maybe heading over there in the new year, and, who knows, just seeing where it goes from there."

"How much money have you given her?"

He took a breath and wiped his nose. "I haven't added it all up. Seven grand? I don't know."

I didn't say anything. My heart was beating hard. I wasn't sure why. Minutes went by and neither of us spoke. "So, Stephen—" I finally said. But right then, he sat up and cocked an ear. "Hush," he whispered, fussing with the rifle. When he managed to lever a round into the chamber, he raised the gun to his shoulder and drew a bead on the far side of the clearing.

"There's nothing there," I said.

He fired, and then charged off into the brush. I let him go. The shot summoned George. He jogged into the clearing just as Stephen was emerging from the scrub.

"Hit something, little brother?" George asked him.

"Guess not," he said.

"At least you got a look," he said. "Next time."

At noon, we climbed back in the boat. There wasn't another craft in sight, and the loveliness of the day was enough to knock you down, but it was lost on me. The picture of gaunt Stephen, panting at his monitor as his sweetheart pumped and squatted for him, her meter ticking merrily, was a final holocaust on my already ravaged mood. I couldn't salvage any of the low glee I've wrung in the past from my brother's misfortunes. Instead, I had a close, clammy feeling that my brother and I were turning into a very ugly pair of men. We'd traced such different routes, each disdaining the other as an emblem of what we were not, only to fetch up, together, in the far weird wastes of life.

The boat plowed on. No planes disturbed the sky. Swallows rioted above the calm green lid of the lake. Birch trees gleamed like filaments among the evergreens. I was dead to it, though I did take a kind of comfort in the fact that all of this beauty was out here, persisting like mad, whether you hearkened to it or not.

George steered us to another stretch of lakefront woods, and I went and hunkered alone in a blueberry copse. My hands were cold, and my thighs and toes were cold, and my cabin would be cold when I got back, and to take a hot shower I would have to heat a kettle on the stove and pour the water into the rubber bladder hanging over my bathtub. The shower in my house in Charleston was a state-of-the-art five-nozzler that simultaneously blasted your face, breasts, and crotch. The fun was quickly going out of this, not just the day, but the whole bit up here, the backbreaking construction hassles, and this bullshit, too—crouching in a wet shrub, masquerading as a rugged hardscrabbler just to maintain the affection of an aged drunk.

Off to my right, I could hear George coughing a wet, complicated, old-man's cough, loud enough to send even the deafest herd galloping for the hills. I leaned out of my bush to scowl at him. He sat swabbing his pitted scarlet nose with a hard green hankie, and disgust and panic overwhelmed me. Where was I? Three months of night were coming on! Stuck in a six-hundred-square-foot crate! I'd probably look worse than the old man when the days got long again! Sell the truck! Sell the cabin! Get a Winnebago! Drive it where?

The sun was sinking when George called out, and the three of us slogged back to the soggy delta where we'd tied the boat.

Glancing down the beach, I spotted something that I thought at first might be a driftwood sculpture, but which sharpened under my stare into the brown serrations of a moose's rack. It was standing in the shallows, its head bent to drink. Well over three hundred yards, and the moose was downwind, probably getting ready to bolt in a second. I was tired. I raised my gun. George started bitching at me.

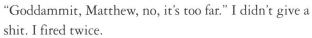 "Goddammit, Matthew, no, it's too far." I didn't give a shit. I fired twice.

The moose's forelegs crumpled beneath it, and an instant later I saw the animal's head jerk as the sound of the shot reached him. The moose tried to struggle upright but fell again. The effect was of a very old person trying to pitch a heavy tent. It tried to stand, and fell, and tried, and fell, and then quit its strivings.

We gazed at the creature piled up down there. Finally, George turned to me, gawping and shaking his head. "That, my friend," he said, "has got to be the goddamnedest piece of marksmanship I've ever seen."

Stephen laughed. "Unreal," he said. He moved to hug me, but he was nervous about my rifle, and he just kind of groped my elbow in an awkward way.

The moose had collapsed in a foot of icy water and had to be dragged onto firm ground before it could be dressed. I waded out to where it lay and Stephen plunged along after me.

We had to crouch and soak ourselves to get the rope under its chest. The other end we looped around a hemlock on the bank, and then tied the rope to the stern of the skiff, using the tree as a makeshift pulley. George gunned the outboard, and Stephen and I stood calf-deep in the shallows heaving on the line. By the time we'd gotten the moose to shore, our palms were torn and puckered, and our boots were full of water.

With George's hunting knife, I bled the moose from the throat, and then made a slit from the bottom of the ribcage to the jaw, revealing the gullet and a pale, corrugated column of windpipe. The scent was powerful. It brought to mind the dark, briny smell that seemed always to hang around my mother in summertime when I was a child.

George was in a rapture, giddy at how I'd put us both in six months of meat with my preposterous shot. "We'll winter well on this," he kept saying. He took the knife from me and gingerly opened the moose's belly, careful not to puncture the intestines or the sack of his stomach. He dragged out the organs, setting aside the liver, the kidneys, and the pancreas. One strange hitch was the hide, which was hellish to remove. To get it loose, Stephen and I had to take turns, bracing our boots against the moose's spine, pulling at the hide while George slashed away at the fascia and connective tissues. I saw Stephen's throat buck nauseously every now and again, yet he wanted to have a part in dressing it, and I was proud of him for that. He took up the game saw and cut off a shoulder and a ham. We had to lift the legs like pallbearers to get them to the boat. Blood ran from the meat and down my shirt with hideous, vital warmth.

The skiff sat low under the weight of our haul. The most substantial ballast of our crew, I sat in the stern and ran the kicker so the bow wouldn't swamp. Stephen sat on the cross bench, our knees nearly touching. We puttered out, a potent blue vapor bubbling up from the propeller. Clearing the shallows, I opened the throttle, and the craft bullied its way through the low swells, a fat white fluke churning up behind us. We skimmed out while the sun sank behind the dark spruce spires in the west. The gridded rubber handle of the Evinrude thrummed in my palm. The wind dried the fluids on my cheeks, and tossed Stephen's hair in a sparse frenzy. With the carcass receding behind us, it seemed I'd also escaped the blackness that had plagued me since Stephen's arrival. The return of George's expansiveness, the grueling ordeal of the butchery, the exhaustion in my limbs, the satisfaction in having made an unreasonably good shot that would feed my friend and me until the snow melted—it was glorious. I could feel absolution spread across the junk-pit of my troubles as smoothly and securely as a motorized tarp slides across a swimming pool.

And Stephen felt it, too, or something anyway. The old unarmored smile I knew from childhood brightened his haunted face, a tidy, compact bow of lip and tooth, alongside which I always looked dour and shabby in the family photographs. There's no point in trying to describe the love I can still feel for my brother when he looks at me this way, when he's stopped tallying his resentments against me and he's briefly left off hating himself for failing to hit the big time as the next John Tesh. Ours isn't the kind of brotherhood

I would wish on other men, but we are blessed with a single, simple gift: in these rare moments of happiness, we can share joy as passionately and single-mindedly as we do hatred. As we skimmed across the dimming lake, I could see how much it pleased him to see me at ease, to have his happiness magnified in my face and reflected back at him. No one said anything. This was love for us, or the best that love could do. I brought the boat in wide around the isthmus guarding the cove, letting the wake push us through the shallows to the launch where my sturdy blue truck was waiting for us.

With the truck loaded, and the skiff rinsed clean, we rode back to the mountain. It was past dinnertime when we reached my place. Our stomachs were yowling.

I asked George and Stephen if they wouldn't mind getting started butchering the meat while I put a few steaks on the grill. George said that before he did any more work he was going to need to sit in a dry chair for a little while and drink two beers. He and Stephen sat and drank and I waded into the bed of my pickup, which was heaped nearly flush with meat. It was disgusting work rummaging in there. George came over and pointed out the short ribs and told me how to hack out the tenderloin, a tapered log of flesh that looked like a peeled boa constrictor. I held it up. George raised his can in tribute. "Now there's a pretty, pretty thing," he said.

I carried the loin to the porch and cut it into steaks two inches thick, which I patted with kosher salt and coarse pepper. I got the briquettes going while George and Stephen blocked out the meat on a plywood-and-sawhorse table in the headlights of my truck.

When the coals had grayed over, I dropped the steaks onto the grill. After ten minutes, they were still good and pink in the center, and I plated them with yellow rice. Then I opened up a bottle of burgundy I'd been saving and poured three glasses. I was about to call the boys to the porch when I saw that something had caused George to halt his labors. A grimace soured his features. He sniffed at his sleeve, then his knife, then the mound of meat in front of him. He winced, took a second careful whiff and recoiled.

"Oh good Christ, it's turning," he said. With an urgent stride, he made for the truck and sprang onto the tailgate, taking up pieces of our kill and putting them to his face. "Son of a bitch," he said. "It's going off, all of it. Contaminated. It's something deep in the meat."

I walked over. I sniffed at the ham he'd been working on. It was true, there was a slight pungency to it, a diarrheal tang gathering in the air, but only faintly. If the intestines had leaked a little, it certainly wasn't any reason to toss thousands of dollars' worth of meat. And anyway, I had no idea how moose flesh was supposed to smell.

"It's just a little gamy," I said. "That's why they call it game."

Stephen smelled his hands. "George is right. It's spoiled. *Gah.*"

"Not possible," I said. "This thing was breathing three hours ago. There's nothing wrong with it."

"It was sick," said George. "That thing was dying on its feet when you shot it."

"Bullshit," I said.

"Contaminated, I promise you," said George. "I should have known it when the skin hung on there like it did. He was bloating up with something, just barely holding on. The second he died, and turned that infection loose, it just started going wild."

Stephen looked at the meat strewn across the table, and at the three of us standing there. Then he began to laugh. I went to the porch and bent over a steaming steak. It smelled fine. I rubbed the salt crust and licked at the juice from my thumb.

"There's nothing wrong with it," I said.

I cut off a dripping pink cube and touched it to my tongue. Stephen was still laughing.

"You're a fucking star, Matty," he said, breathless. "All the beasts in the forest, and you mow down a leper moose. God, that smell. Don't touch that shit, man. Call in a hazmat team."

"There's not a goddamned thing wrong with this meat," I said.

"Poison," said George.

The wind gusted suddenly. A branch fell in the woods. A squad of leaves scurried past my boots and settled against the door. Then the night went still again. I turned back to my plate and slipped the fork into my mouth.

CATHERINE BUSSINGER has been published in several literary journals. She lives in Berkeley with her husband and son.

MICHAEL CERA was born in Brampton, Ontario, and now lives in Los Angeles. "Pinecone" is his first published story.

BILL COTTER lives in Austin with the poet Annie La Ganga. His first novel, *Fever Chart*, will be published by McSweeney's this summer.

NICK EKKIZOGLOY is a native South Georgian now living in Northern Virginia. He recently received an MFA from the University of Montana, and has since been working in the warehouse of a major retailer. He is also working on a novel. "Stowaways" is his first published story.

J. MALCOLM GARCIA's work has appeared in *The Best American Travel Writing* and *The Best American Non-Required Reading*.

SHARI GERSTENBERGER studied Comparative Literature at Colorado College. For her senior thesis she translated Matei Visniec's *L'homme poubelle*, excerpts of which appear in English for the first time here. She currently lives in Austin.

ETGAR KERET has published several story collections, including *The Nimrod Flipout* and *The Girl on the Fridge*. His books have been translated into twenty-four languages. *Jellyfish*, a film co-directed by Keret and his wife, Shira Geffen, won the Camera d'Or prize at the 2007 Cannes Film Festival.

CARSON MELL has lived in Hollywood, California for the last six years, writing and making short films. His work has screened at Sundance, CineVegas, the San Francisco International Film Festival, can be seen on every odd-numbered issue of *Wholphin*. His first novel, *Saguaro*, is available through his web site, www.carsonmell.com.

KEVIN MOFFETT is the author of *Permanent Visitors*, a collection of stories. He lives in Claremont, California.

SHELLY ORIA was born in Los Angeles and grew up in Israel; she earned her MFA from Sarah Lawrence College in 2007. Her fiction has appeared in *Quarterly West*, *LIT*, and the *Spectrum Anthology*. She is currently completing her first story collection, *New York 1, Tel Aviv 0*, the title story of which was the recipient of the *Indiana Review*'s 2008 fiction prize.

WELLS TOWER's first story collection, *Everything Ravaged, Everything Burned*, will be published this spring by Farrar, Straus, and Giroux in the United States and Canada, and by Granta Books in the United Kingdom.

MATEI VISNIEC was born in Romania in 1956; he began writing for the theater in 1977. During the following ten years, he wrote some twenty plays, all of which were banned by the Romanian censors. In 1987, after being brought to France by a literary foundation, he asked for political asylum. Since then, his work has been staged in more than fifteen countries. He is now one of the most-performed playwrights in Romania.

(cont. from copyright page) An emotional niggardliness seemed to pervade the story. A brief synopsis might have read, "A smug narrator perceives his brother to be obnoxious, and his perceptions are ratified when his brother ultimately ingests a ration of possibly lethal moose flesh." The story aspired to stingy ends, a kind of glib, just-deserts satisfaction at best. The stuff I'd liked most, the gag lines perpetrated by the Bob character, looked on second glance like a bunch of shucking and jiving: ha-cha-cha-cha! You could hear where the rimshots were supposed to go. ¶One question a smart teacher of mine liked to ask in fiction workshops is, "Was this written in good faith?" I took this to mean: did the writer make himself as vulnerable to the story's possibilities as he wishes his readers to be? Or, more simply put: does the writer believe in what he wrote? That first draft, with the bitter younger brother narrating, felt like it flunked the good-faith test. ¶So I took another stab at it, tasking myself with a mission of greater narrative generosity, a more complicated balance of sympathies, fewer cheap tricks. In order to liberate Matthew, the older brother, from his simple role as a bungling blowhard, it seemed necessary to let him tell the tale. It struck me as a sadder and more interesting story if we could get to know Matthew as a plenary human being, an aware, discerning narrator who nonetheless can't stop alienating people despite what he believes are his best intentions. I worked on that idea for about two months, hammering, hammering at the human-sympathy forge. When I proudly started passing the draft around, the editor of my collection, and a few others I showed it to, sort of shrugged and went *Eh*. The new draft wasn't as funny. Matthew had become too sympathetic, too verbally capable, too *written*, plus I'd crammed on a sentimental new ending that didn't work. I felt sick at heart. So much for magnanimity. ¶But then on a second read, my editor decided that there might be some promise in the new draft after all. She had the bright idea of borrowing a bit or two from the first draft, purging some of the verbal algae blooms I'd clotted the pages with, and trimming the mawkish closer. After another few weeks' worth of work, we had a story we both felt okay about. ¶It may be the case that the first draft, the younger-brother one, is the more successful story. Nevertheless, I prefer the second. It feels to me as though it grapples harder with our universal tendency to vex ourselves. Or, at the very least, the last time I read it, I didn't get that sinking, face-in-the-mirror feeling, which is enough for me for now. ¶My only real regret about the story is that I wasn't able to slip in another fine piece of moose lore I picked up in Alaska. One day, as I was getting ready to push off on a kayak trip across a big cold lake on the Kenai Peninsula, a park ranger came over and told me to beware of swimming moose. It was rut season, when the bulls go crazy. They'll put a hoof through your boat in a second, the ranger told me, just for the fun of it. But the really interesting thing he said was that when he's in rut, a bull moose standing on one side of the lake might suddenly get a very strong hunch that a cow moose is waiting for him on the far side of the lake, which might be as much as two or three miles away (these are big lakes). Off he'll swim. But when he's just about gotten to the distant shore, he'll take a contrary notion that, actually, all the ladies are probably on the shore he just swam from. So he does an about-face and paddles back the way he came. Just as the moose is finally reaching terra firma, he doubts himself again, and again with the U-turn. A lot of moose, the ranger said, kill themselves this way. As I was revising and revising this story and others, I thought often about those indecisive, waterlogged creatures. As much as I believe in the radical rewrite, I hope that someday I'll get better at picking a single course and sticking with it. The pond is always bigger than it looks. INTERNS & VOLUNTEERS: Kathleen Alcott, Sandra Allen, April Goldman, Chelsea Cox, Joannna Green, Juliet Litman, Alex Ludlum, Ling Ma, Kyle O'Loughlin, Lindsay Quella, Arianna Reiche, Megan Rickel, Eric Vennemeyer, Bennet Bergman, Royanne Curtin, Josh Freydkis, Graham Haught, Michael Sisskin, Cassandra Neyenesch, Christina Rush, Benjamin Jahn. ALSO HELPING: Alvaro Villanueva, Chris Ying, Michelle Quint, Brian McMullen, Eliana Stein, Greg Larson, Jesse Nathan, Christopher Benz. COPY EDITORS: Oriana Leckert, Caitlin Van Dusen. WEBSITE: Chris Monks, Ed Page. SUPPORT: Darren Franich. OUTREACH: Angela Petrella. CIRCULATION: Heidi Meredith. MANAGING EDITOR: Jordan Bass. PUBLISHER: Eli Horowitz. EDITOR: Dave Eggers.

INTERIOR ART: Jason Polan.